The Ghosts of Littletown

Book One:

The Dreamer

Matthew G. McMillan

This is a work of fiction. Names, characters, places, and incidents are products of the author's imagination or are used fictitiously. Any resemblance to actual events or locales or persons, living or dead, is entirely coincidental.

Previously published by
Authors and Artists Publishers of New York
As "The Dreamer" © 2002 Matthew G. McMillan

The Ghosts of Littletown Book One: The Dreamer (2nd edition)
© 2018 Matthew G. McMillan. All rights reserved.
ISBN – 978-0-359-13295-9
Printed in the United States of America

Category: Young Adult Fantasy

Book Design: Matthew G. McMillan
Front Cover Art: Matthew G. McMillan/SK Cothren
Back Cover Photo: SK Cothren

BOOKS BY MATTHEW G. MCMILLAN

THE GHOSTS OF LITTLETOWN

BOOK ONE: THE DREAMER

BOOK TWO: THE SEVEN

(HORROR SHORT FICTION)

HAUNTS AND SLIPSTREAMS

<u>Special Thanks to:</u>

SK Cothren and

Lisa Jacoby

-This one is for Matt G

Who never gave up,

Was willing to go back in time,

Walk the road through Raflure in the dark,

Face the demons,

Find old friends,

And set things right.

Mysterious things happen in our

World all the time –

In the secret places

Between our dreams and our minds

There is a small town

Where mysterious things happen rather frequently –

A town between here and there...

Prologue

"I have not been able to sense Mother Nature recently," the Creator said in a slightly detached voice. "It feels like a part of me is missing. I am connected to all five of my Keepers and this is the *first* time that I have ever felt like one of you is *lost*."

Father Time listened. He had been watching the sunrise from the ruins of an ancient stone temple in The Realm of Timeless Wisdom when the Creator had appeared and began telling him that something had gone wrong. He often had visits from the Creator, but this was the first time the Creator had come to him with an issue about one of the Keepers possibly being in danger.

"You cannot locate her with your power?" Father Time asked, rubbing his thumb on his wooden staff. He was unsure of what the Creator wanted from him. The Worlds and Realms had their troubles, but this *did* feel like something new – something far more dangerous than anything he had been part of before. And he'd been around for a long time, since the beginning. The future was something he could not clearly see.

"I do not have the ability to find her *now*," the Creator replied, sounding upset and slightly confused. "I think her crystal sphere is malfunctioning. Or, maybe she has been separated from it." The Creator paused. "Using the pocket watches to test for those worthy of becoming Dream Walkers was a good idea. However, we have lost the first Dream Walker: and the next *four* did not survive their quests. Seven watches of power – and not *one* surviving Dream Walker to show for it."

Father Time was aware of the failure to find beings capable of becoming Dream Walkers – individuals strong enough to be warriors for the Creator and the Keepers. He had been there at the failure of the last attempt. Such a terrible end the unicorn had met. Even with the ability to move matter with her mind, it had not been enough to save her from being drowned by water demons. He had been powerless to save her, as his purpose was to govern time.

His thoughts drifted to his fellow Keepers. They rarely came together, even though they were the Creator's pillars for holding existence in place. Mother Nature Traveled the Worlds and Realms tending to life. Death took the essences of the dead to their next destination – or, in extreme cases, ended the essence altogether. The Gate Keeper kept watch in his Gateway Hall as beings Traveled between Worlds and Realms. Father Time did his duty to allow change and growth in the Worlds and Realms, while Medusa, the Dream Keeper, ruled over the spaces in between the Worlds and Realms: she was the embodiment of what it was to dream, to explore the unknown. They worked as individuals, not as a unit. If one was gone, what would happen? Would all things be thrown into chaos?

"There are others who will be worthy of becoming Dream Walkers,"

Father Time said. "We know that they will work things out, just not when. Or how."

"I did not *plan* at the beginning. I still cannot," the Creator said evenly. "I create. Life. Death. Time. Dreams. Beings. Worlds. Realms. Perhaps it is time I take a larger role in what happens in my creation. Let us find someone to search for Mother Nature and bring her a new crystal sphere!"

There was a brilliant flash of light and a sphere appeared on the stone table beside Father Time. It was a little larger than a softball, murky for a moment as if smoke was billowing inside the clear ball, but it cleared after a couple of seconds. The crystal sphere glistened in the morning sunlight. A second later it returned to its murky state, looking dull and rather insignificant.

"I have had my eye on Jack Parker's daughter, Molly" the Creator said thoughtfully. "Perhaps she is ready to become a Dream Walker."

Chapter One

It was a cold October evening in Littletown. Dusk had fallen, and a cold breeze rustled the few leaves still clinging to the trees. It was a crisp sound, as the leaves were dry and brittle. Molly Parker walked along Main Street, her arms hugging a stack of books close to her chest. She jumped, startled, as the library bell began to chime the hour. Molly shook her head, mentally scolding herself for being jumpy as she approached the stone library that stood a few yards from Main Street. It was a converted old church, erected in town more than two hundred years ago, when the town had been settled. Color cardboard cutouts of pumpkins and black cats adorned the windows facing the road. The library was closed. At the top of the steps, by the front door, was the book return bin. Molly scampered up the steps, dumped the books in, and hurried back down to the sidewalk. The sixth bell chimed and fell silent.

The cars that passed by were mostly older models: some quite rusty and in need of serious repair. One of the passing cars honked at Molly, startling her again, but it was too far down the road for her to see the make of the car or the driver.

"Thanks for nothing, dork!" she muttered, angry at being startled twice in a matter of seconds.

The businesses and houses along Main Street were rustic, yet homey and peaceful. The lights that glowed softly from the windows and streetlights gave a kind of warmth to the cold evening.

Molly hurried up the steps of Sandra's Place, a couple of buildings down Main Street from the library. She glanced at a jack-o'-lantern on the porch, next to the front door. The pumpkin wasn't lit. It would be in a few days, when Halloween night arrived. Molly opened the door to Sandra's hair salon and slipped inside.

As the two occupants turned to see who had entered, Molly smiled shyly with her head tilted slightly down, eyes on her well-worn sneakers.

Molly did not lack self-confidence, but sometimes when she went out she became self-aware and wanted to withdraw. For some reason, this was one of those times. She knew that she was pretty, with her smooth skin, long dark brown hair, and clear grey eyes behind wire-framed glasses. Yet, she also knew that who she really was inside didn't always come out the way she felt that it should. She knew that she looked good in jeans – she had stood looking at herself in the mirror often enough, twisting her hips to make sure her butt and the jeans worked well together. Even the thick sweater she wore did little to take away from her attractiveness. She wasn't popular in school, but she didn't really care. There was a part of her that wanted to fit in, but she didn't bother making the effort. She spent time hanging out with her friends, but also spent a lot of time doing things alone in her room. However, like most of the teenage girls she knew, she liked boys – one in particular. Brian Carter. He was the brother of her friend, Cindy Carter. They had all known each other since they were toddlers. Brian was one year older than her. She'd kissed him a couple of years ago, and even though nothing had come of it. She'd been hoping that *something* would.

Sandra, the owner, head stylist, and the only one who appeared to be working that night, as usual, looked up from her current client and said, "Hello, Molly!"

"Hello," Molly replied softly.

"It'll only be a minute – take a seat!" Sandra said in her friendly manner.

Molly sat down in a chair by the large window that faced Main Street. The place smelled of hair treatments – and something else that she couldn't quite figure out, something she had never smelled in Sandra's Place before. It was kind of like the smoke that came from a burned-out electrical appliance, but a little sweeter and not as acidic. It was faint and she didn't bother asking about it.

While she waited, Molly leafed through a women's magazine, skimming the articles, until the lady getting her hair done was finished. The lady looked familiar, but Molly didn't know her name. She smiled at Molly as she left.

"You're up, Molly!" Sandra called out as she shook out the plastic sheet used to catch hair clippings.

"The usual?" Sandra asked.

Molly nodded. She liked her hair long and straight so she could easily pull it into a ponytail. "Yeah," she said, glad to be the only one beside Sandra in the hair salon. "Am I your last one tonight?" Molly asked.

"Closing up after we're done," Sandra replied, looking at Molly's reflection in the large mirror. "No appointments after six! Then I can go home and eat. I'm starving!"

Molly smiled. She took her glasses off and set them on the counter in front of her. As Sandra began to spray down her hair, Molly turned to look out the window facing Main Street.

A young girl was walking on the sidewalk. She looked in at Molly and waved a hand wearing a thick red mitten. Molly couldn't see very clearly from that distance without her glasses, although she could see well enough to know that she didn't recognize the girl. Molly pulled a hand out from under the plastic sheet and waved back anyway. It was a small town and almost everyone knew everyone, or at least knew about them.

Sandra looked out the window as Molly waved. "A friend of yours?" she asked.

"No," answered Molly.

The child dropped her hand and skipped out of view.

Probably one of those elementary kids who looks up to us high-schoolers, Molly thought.

Sandra and Molly chatted as Sandra worked. Nothing special, but it passed the time. Twenty minutes later, Molly left with shorter hair and less money.

As she walked home, she could see the moon rising large and bright on the horizon. It was like a moon out of one of those cheesy horror flicks she watched with her friends, and she almost believed that she might hear a wolf howling in the distance. But no wolves were howling tonight. She walked quickly, telling herself that it was because of the cold evening and not because Halloween was in three days and wolves (or maybe even werewolves) might be lurking about.

Most of the buildings along Main Street were businesses and they were decorated for the autumn holiday. Little white ghosts hung from trees and paper skeletons posed in windows.

A police car siren blared and its red and blue lights flashed from behind her, causing her to jump. She chided herself again for being jumpy as the police car pulled over a rusty pick-up truck on the other side of Main Street. The flashing lights danced and reflected off the many surfaces around her. As she reached the spot where they had pulled over, she recognized the officer in the police car. It was Tony Andrews, her friend Candice's father, darkly clad in his uniform. He didn't notice her as he got out of his squad car and walked up to the driver in the rusty pick-up. He clicked on his flashlight and aimed it in at the driver. Molly could overhear what they were saying, and she watched the scene out of the corner of her eye as she walked.

"Good evening," Tony told the driver. "Did you see the speed limit sign back there?"

Molly could see the young man behind the wheel of the battered truck as he looked at Tony with a guilt-ridden face. "Sorry, sir," he mumbled.

It was Ralph Little. He was a nice enough guy, a few years older than Molly, and she thought he was kind of cute. However, she didn't find Ralph very interesting and, therefore, not someone she had gotten know. He had graduated last year and worked stocking shelves at the grocery store in town. He was one of the descendants of the family that settled Littletown back in the late 1700's. The family owned the grocery store, the bowling alley, and the lumberyard that was on the edge of town.

She kept walking, passing out of earshot, until she reached the main intersection in town. There were a few stoplights around town, but most of the traffic in Littletown came through this spot. There weren't many cars on the road on this particular night. She crossed easily, passing the church on the corner, and turned up the walkway of the apartment building next to it. Molly and her mother lived in the ground floor apartment on the left side, closest to the church. She hopped up the steps and went inside.

Molly's mother, Karla Parker, had been fighting a cold for a couple of days. She was propped up on the sofa sipping tea and listening to the radio. Her dark brown hair had not been washed since she'd come down with her illness and her nose was red and sore from repeatedly blowing her nose.

"Oh, Mom!" Molly groaned sympathetically. "Is there anything I can get you? Some soup, maybe?"

"That would be great!" Karla replied in a nasal voice. She managed a smile. "Your hair looks nice."

Molly smiled, reached up to touch it, and said, "It's the same as I usually get. Thanks, though. I'll heat up some chicken soup. Be right back!"

"In the cupboard by the refrigerator," her mother said as Molly entered the kitchen.

"I got it," Molly replied. She knew where everything in the kitchen was.

A few minutes later, Molly entered the living room with a steaming bowl of chicken noodle soup and a compassionate smile. "It's still really hot," Molly warned. "You might want to let it cool down a bit first."

"That's kind of you," Karla said. "Did you make some for yourself?"

Molly set the bowl down beside the box of tissues on the coffee table. "Yeah," she said, heading back into the kitchen to get hers.

The living room, like the rest of the apartment, was not overly furnished: just one sofa, a coffee table, two cushioned chairs, a small TV on a stand, and two small coffee tables. Molly sat in the chair opposite her mother, a bowl of soup firmly in her hands.

There was a moment where both of them blew on their soup and sipped a little broth.

"So," Molly started to ask hesitantly, looking down at her soup, "what are we going to do about Halloween this year?"

Karla shrugged and stirred her soup for a moment.

"Are we going to go out?" Molly asked, looking up from her soup.

"I haven't decided yet," her mother said quietly. "Is there something you'd like to do?"

"Well, if you're not feeling well, we can stay home..." Molly offered. "We don't have to give out candy or anything." She paused to spoon a bit of soup.

"Maybe we will," Karla said, sounding uncertain. "We've still got a few days to decide. But maybe we should go out to eat or something. I don't know if I want to sit around here. We'll figure something out."

"Okay," Molly agreed. "Whatever you decide will be fine with me."

After Karla was done with her soup, Molly took the empty bowls into the kitchen and refilled her mother's teacup. Then she went to her room to start her homework.

Molly sat down on her bed and sighed heavily. *I wish Dad was here,* she thought sadly. She looked around her room. Hanging on the walls around her were posters of kittens, horses, her favorite movies, and one of her favorite band. Between them hung a few medals she had won for her long-distance runs with the Littletown track team. What meant most to her was not that she'd won them, but that her father had been there for every single race.

There was a painting (the only artwork on the walls that she hadn't made herself) that her father had given to her for her birthday six years ago. It was of Littletown in autumn, looking down Main Street with the hills in the background. The leaves on the trees were beautiful shades of red and orange. Her Dad had said that it was a special painting, but Molly had always thought it was a strange gift to give a young girl – especially since she'd gotten a stuffed unicorn, a bunch of Nancy Drew books, red glitter slippers, and candy from her parents on that same birthday.

She looked over at the bookshelf that was full of Nancy Drew mysteries, over two dozen fantasy books, and some of her favorite kid's books she'd kept from her childhood. There were trinkets and cute toys in front of some of the books.

Suddenly, her eyes shot back to the painting of Littletown. Molly gasped in surprise, putting a hand over her mouth. A shiver ran through her. For a brief instant, there had been a Centaur standing on the street in the painting!

It was not there now as she was staring at the painting, but Molly was certain that a Centaur – human from the waist up, horse from the waist down – had just been in it!

She dropped her hand and slowly pushed herself up. She walked over to the painting. She reached out and touched it – dry paint, nothing more. She took a deep breath.

Now I'm hallucinating! she thought.

But she had seen it! Hadn't she?

Molly sat down at her desk, shaking her head and smiling nervously. *You're not crazy, Molly!* she assured herself. *You're just seeing things. Jumping at nothing again.* But she couldn't shake the image of the Centaur, which was now etched clearly in her memory. She *had* seen it!

She sat at the desk doing her homework, looking up at the painting nearly every minute hoping to see the image again. She did not. Later that night, she tossed and turned in bed. It took her almost two hours to fall asleep…

Molly was standing in swirling, falling snow. It was night, the only source of light coming from the streetlights along the road. And she could only see a few of them – the others were lost in the thick snowflakes

I'm dreaming, she thought, looking around at the falling snow. She was standing at the front door of her apartment, looking out toward Main Street. She stepped out from under the overhang above the door and into the foot of snow on the ground as she made her way to the sidewalk. The wind was blowing hard and the snow was a curtain of white. She couldn't see the house across the street or the church on the corner to her right.

She was cold. She crossed her arms over her chest and looked down. Her feet were bare. So were her legs. *Oh, great, a naked dream!* she thought. *Figures I'd be naked in a snowstorm.*

"What's next?" she asked aloud. *And where can I get some clothes?* her brain added.

She started walking down the sidewalk, heading for the intersection on Main Street. She turned to look behind her. Her apartment building had vanished! *Well*, she thought, *I guess I'm not going home*. With the streetlights as her only guide in this winter nightmare-land, she reached the spot where the stoplight should have been, but found no road, no stoplight, nor any buildings: just a foot of snow on the ground all around her, with the soft lights above in the heavy snowfall.

"Molly!" a youthful voice called out.

Molly jumped, turning to face the voice. A young girl was standing a few yards away. The girl was bundled up for the snowy weather, holding out a hand in a thick red mitten.

"Take my hand, Molly," the girl said with a big smile. She looked about seven years old, and kind of like the girl she'd seen wave to her at Sandra's in the waking world.

Molly was hugging herself, shivering. She couldn't see the young girl's eyes very well under the thick hat that the girl wore. The girl's bangs were thick, also helping to obscure her eyes.

"I'm cold," she said, her teeth starting to chatter. "This dream sucks."

"You are lost," the girl said sympathetically. "I can take you to where it is warm, and where you will be safe."

Molly reached out as she stepped forward and clasped the small hand in the red knitted mitten. The girl led Molly through the snow. A few seconds later Molly could make out something ahead, a small mound of grass rising up from the snow.

"What is it?" Molly asked, thinking it looked like a huge reverse snow-globe.

"A place of warmth," the girl replied in a louder voice without turning her head.

Molly could see clearly now. Light was emanating from the grassy mound. A clear bubble covered the mound so that no snow could get in. A pole with a white banner was at the top of the mound. The word "ABEYANCE" was written in golden letters on the banner. The girl effortlessly penetrated the bubble and stepped on the grass, pulling Molly in with her. Instantly, Molly was warm and she no longer cared that she was naked. She felt more comfortable here than any place she had been in the real world.

Molly stood, looking up, watching as the snowflakes slid off of the clear dome above her. "What is this place?" she asked.

The girl let go of Molly's hand and spoke as she walked up to the pole with the banner at the top. "This is an in-between place," she said. "A place to find comfort, a place of peace. But when you leave here, you must be prepared. You must have what you need to endure. You will need clothes…"

Clothing materialized on the grass beside the pole.

"You will also need food and drink," the girl with the red mittens added.

A canteen materialized beside the clothes, along with a pouch on a leather strap.

"But I don't *want* to go back out there!" Molly protested loudly.

The girl laughed – a most beautiful laugh, full of innocent amusement – then said, as if it were obvious, "But you *must* go back out there!"

The scene vanished and Molly was left alone in the snowstorm again. The girl with the red mittens, the grass mound, the bubble, and banner were gone. The clothes, canteen, and pouch still lay on the ground. The falling snow began to cover them.

As Molly reached down to pick up the clothes, she heard the girl repeat, "But you *must* go back out there!"

Molly's alarm clock was screeching as she awoke with a start. Throwing the covers aside, she crossed the room to shut it off. She had placed the alarm clock on her desk so that she would *have* to get out of bed to turn it off. It was too easy to reach out from under the covers, tap the "off" button, and go back to sleep. She'd done it more than once before.

She put her glasses on and stumbled sleepily into the kitchen. She got out a box of cereal and put it on the table while she got out the milk and orange juice. The coffee maker was going already. Her mother had set it to auto-drip the night before as usual. Her mother walked in sleepy-eyed as Molly started in on breakfast.

"Good morning, sweetie," Karla said with a groggy smile. "Sleep well?"

"Weird dream," Molly replied, pouring herself a glass of orange juice.

15

"But I think I got some sleep." She was thinking not just about her oddly vivid dream, but also the Centaur she'd seen in the painting last night. She was close with her mother, but not sure she wanted to go into her possible delusions this early in the day – or ever.

Karla flipped on the radio that was next to the toaster. It was set on a station that played light music and gave regular news and weather updates. It wasn't bad music, but Molly preferred music that rocked a little more. The weather forecaster was on, talking about how it would be warm for this time of year. Maybe even be in the 60's for Halloween.

Molly noticed that her mother's nose was a lighter shade of red this morning, almost pink, as Karla poured herself a mug of coffee. A rather large mug, too. Molly was glad to see her mother's thirst for coffee back up to normal standards; perhaps a little more so.

Molly's brain was still playing over the girl's words from her dream, "But you *must* go back out there!"

"Yeah," Molly said to her mother, "I had a strange dream last night."

Karla sat down at the table beside her daughter. "Tell me about it," she said. She listened with interest as Molly related the dream of the girl with red mittens, the grass mound, and the snowstorm. After a thoughtful moment, Karla said, "That *is* quite a dream!" She could tell that it was taking up almost all of Molly's attention, as if her daughter had not been able to quite wake up from the dream yet. "Do you think it means anything?"

"I'm not sure, but it feels like…I don't know…like it's *supposed* to mean something," Molly said, thinking hard. "I don't know. It's too early." Her mother agreed. Molly ate. Her mother listened to the music and sipped her coffee. A couple of minutes later, Molly looked up at the clock. It was almost seven. "I need to take a shower and get ready for school." She got up to put her breakfast stuff away. "What do *you* think about the dream?" she asked over her shoulder.

"It could mean something," her mother said, tilting her head and shrugging a little. "Or, maybe nothing." She paused to sniff. "Think about it, maybe something will come to you. Too bad your father wasn't here." Her eyes grew watery. "He'd know."

Molly paused as she was putting the milk and orange juice back in the refrigerator. She knew that they would have talk about him soon, but didn't want to do it now. She missed him as much as her mother did.

"I need to get ready, too," Karla said, wiping her eyes and standing up quickly.

Molly was glad her mother had dropped the topic of her father. She put the cartons on the top shelf in the refrigerator and asked, "Feeling good enough to go to work today?"

"I think I can handle it," Karla said firmly. "Definitely feeling better this morning. I don't want to sit around here all day again. If I start feeling too sick, I can come home early." She smiled at her daughter. It was a look of loving tenderness. "Don't worry, honey, I'm taking care of myself."

Molly returned a smile of her own. "I know. I just don't like seeing you sick."

"I should hope not!" Karla said playfully.

"I love you, Mom," Molly said as she headed down the hall toward the bathroom.

"Love you, too, Molly Margaret!" Karla called out. She used Molly's middle name for two reasons. One – if she was angry with her daughter. Two – as in this case, when she felt especially close to her.

Molly got ready for school and left as her mother was showering. She didn't bother with a jacket since the weather was supposed to be nice. She liked Indian summers. She thought that they were one of the best parts of autumn. The walk to school was only a few blocks and she spent the entire time thinking about the Centaur that had popped into the painting of Littletown that her Dad had given her a few years ago, and her strange dream about the girl in the snowstorm.

What was going on? It reminded her of how things used to be, back when her father was still around. She missed him like crazy. Her mother had been right: if her Dad had been there at the table this morning, he would have been able to tell her if her dream had a deeper meaning.

The loud busses pulling into the school at the front entrance broke her train of thought. She was grateful – she didn't want to start her day crying as she walked into school. She could see the other students streaming into Littletown Junior-Senior High. Some of the students walked in alone, but most were chattering in small groups as Molly joined them. It wasn't a large school. Molly only had forty-seven classmates.

"Molly!" a girl's voice called out from up ahead.

She half-expected it to be that girl with the red mittens – she was sure now that the girl in her dream had been the same one she'd seen at Sandra's Place. However, she recognized the voice that called out to her. It was Cindy Carter, one of her close friends. Brian's sister. Cindy was cutting through the stream of students heading into the school, making her way to Molly.

"Hey, Cindy," said Molly, addressing her friend as they came together. "What's up?"

Cindy did not hide her figure. She wore tight jeans – she wore them as often as possible, unless she was wearing shorts as high up her legs as the school would allow – and a turtleneck a size too small with the sleeves pushed up her arms to her elbows. She was a natural blond, her golden hair hanging loosely around her shoulders. She was well-developed for a fifteen-year-old, and many of the guys passing by gave her a thorough look-over. Molly noticed that some of them were looking at her, too.

"You know Rob, from English and Science class, right?" Cindy asked.

The sounds of shuffling feet, morning conversation, and lockers being opened and closed filled the school halls as the two teens walked through the front doors.

"Yeah," Molly said simply. "Who doesn't?" With less than fifty other people in her grade, she knew every one of them. And not because she wanted to.

The first bell rang. It was loud, but Molly didn't jump.

"Argh! Annoying," Cindy said with a frown. "I've got to get to class, but I'll tell you about Rob today. Maybe at lunch."

With that bit of news delivered, seed planted, she took off. Molly watched as her friend walked gracefully down the crowded hall. Cindy's story about her and Rob wouldn't be a surprise. Molly knew that something was going on between them. It was obvious. Cindy had had similar 'guy stories' last year, their sophomore year. Molly figured that her friend would run out of guys in their grade before they graduated. Her other good friend, Candice, probably wouldn't be too far behind. Molly thought about how she had ended up with friends like them. They weren't bad people, or that different from most girls. Molly simply wanted friends with more imagination, but Littletown was where she lived, and she did the best she could. She genuinely liked Cindy and Candice. They were good friends – and, for better or worse, didn't keep many secrets between the three of them. Molly appreciated their honesty, even if it was about stuff that she wasn't as interested in as they were.

It was a Friday and most of the classes she had that day were full of tests. Molly didn't like tests one bit, but they made the day go by a little faster. Lunch was somewhat chaotic and Cindy had to wait to reveal her BIG news to Molly at the end of the school day.

Cindy was a cheerleader and had to get ready shortly after school (the Littletown Badgers were playing an away game with the Dryden Lions later that evening) so she was waiting by Molly's locker with her arms still holding her stuff from her last class as Molly walked up to her locker.

"You're never going to believe what happened to me last night!" Cindy said as Molly reached out to do her locker combination.

"Then don't tell me," Molly said sarcastically. She knew it was relationship oriented, but sometimes the details *were* interesting.

"Well, Rob came over last night…" Cindy began dreamily, hugging her books and lost in last night's rapture. The after-school Friday rush didn't exist there and she smiled, making Molly slightly uncomfortable. "He's got a great smile. And we almost–" Cindy stopped in mid-sentence, noticing that Molly had ceased trying to open her locker and was staring at her.

"Almost what?" Molly asked. "Had a life-altering conversation about the meaning of life?"

Cindy stared back at Molly with a blank face. She shook her head a little. "Do you want to hear about it, or not?" Cindy asked, used to her friend's sarcasm. She liked making Molly wait, dragging her stories out for as long as possible, partly because she re-lived them in a way that was better than when the things had actually happened, and partly because she knew that it annoyed Molly – who she had never seen with a boy in all the years they'd been in school together.

"Yeah," Molly replied, rolling her eyes. She returned her attention back to her locker combination. It was 16 left, 24 right, and then…

"Seven," said a familiar voice from behind her.

Molly turned to see Cindy's older brother, Brian, standing there with his standard lopsided grin. He was just over a year older than Cindy, in his senior year. His light brown hair was cut short and his dark brown eyes looked at Molly with a mixture of playfulness and nervousness. He was a little lanky, and only an inch taller than Molly. She liked him a lot, more than she'd ever admitted to him or anyone else.

She was about to ask him how he knew the last number of her combination when he started in on his sister. "So, Molly," he said with his contagious grin, "has Cindy told you about *Rob* yet? She was carrying on the whole morning about him. *Rob*, this…*Rob*, that." He waved his right hand back and forth and spoke in a dreamy tone to help Molly understand just how annoying she'd been.

Cindy shook her head back and forth slightly and hugged her books a little tighter. "You don't understand, jerk," she said, narrowing her eyes. "You've never even had a *date*," she said with the nasty tone she saved for her annoying older brother. "Rob's different," she added defensively.

"Yeah, right," Brian said, rolling his eyes and then giving Molly a knowing look. He looked back at his sister. "You said that about Gregg, too. Now you don't even talk to *him*. And he's my best friend."

Molly had heard all this before. She turned back to her locker, stopped it at the number 7, and opened it.

"Whatever," Cindy said to her brother, and then walked away in a huff.

"What do you think about that?" Brian asked Molly.

"How did you know the last number of my combination was 7?"

Brian looked a little nervous. "I'm not sure. Just knew it, I guess."

"You said it like you *knew* it." Molly stated. "Do you usually watch me open my locker or something?" she asked. She kind of hoped he did.

As she was asking him, a strange look crossed his face and his lop-sided grin faded. He looked concerned, his forehead wrinkling. He breathed in deeply and sharply. No one else had noticed.

"Are you alright?" Molly asked quietly.

"I don't..." he shook his head. "I...*saw*...something," Brian said slowly.

"Like the number of my locker combination?"

"No."

"What did you see?" asked Molly. He looked like he'd seen a ghost.

Brian looked around nervously. "You promise to be cool – and not freak out?" His dark brown eyes peered at her sharply.

Molly raised her eyebrows and blushed. "I never told anyone about that time in the closet a couple years ago," she said, a little surprised at her boldness. It had been a brief moment, but it had been her first kiss – her only kiss – and one of the secrets not even Cindy or Candice knew about.

Brian blushed in return. "If Cindy ever found out…"

"Don't worry," Molly said quickly. "She won't! Just tell me what you saw."

Brian nervously worked his tongue in his mouth and glanced around. No one was paying them much attention. It was Friday and school was out. Sporting events, late nights, sleepovers, and Halloween parties were the topic of most conversations. Molly and Brian talking in front of her locker drew no one's attention. Molly waited.

"I saw your father," Brian said finally. "Like he was right here!" His eyes locked with Molly's.

"My what?" asked Molly, thinking that she must have misheard him. She hesitated. "Did you say that you saw…my *father*?"

Brian took a deep breath. "Yeah, like he was standing *right beside* you!"

The hairs on the back of her neck stood up. She could tell that he wasn't joking. She knew him well enough to know that he was being sincere, even if it was a creepy thing to say.

"Oh," she said quietly, and then added, "What am I supposed to say to that? That you just saw… my dad…"

"I'm sorry," Brian pleaded. He shifted his feet in discomfort. "Maybe I'll just go. See you later."

Molly watched him as he walked away. She let him go without trying to call him back. He looked a little scared, and a lot embarrassed. As if it wasn't hard enough to have lost her father on Halloween last year, the one year anniversary seemed to have everything around her pointing right at the one thing that she, and her mother, had struggled to move on from.

"But you *must* go back out there!"

The words came from nowhere, and Molly seemed to be the only one who had heard them. She turned back to her locker to get the stuff she needed for the weekend and walked out of the school as fast as she could – without looking like someone who was seeing things in paintings, having the boy she liked say he saw the spirit of her father a few seconds ago, and someone who heard the voice from a girl she'd seen in a dream the night before.

Dad, Molly thought, *I wish you were here…* The dream with the girl leading her to that grassy mound filled her mind. *The girl said that I would need to have stuff to endure. Does that have something to do with Dad? And what the hell does 'abeyance' mean anyway?*

Molly walked home along the sidewalk, looking up at the hills in the distance. It was almost the same as the painting hanging in her bedroom.

I bet I won't see Cindy much in the next month or two, she thought to herself as her mind raced. She wanted to tell Brian that she liked him and didn't know why she found it so difficult to just say so. Now things were even more complicated after he told her that he'd seen her father like he was a ghost or something. *So why do I feel like he really **did** see Dad?* she asked herself seriously.

There was sudden blast of bitter cold wind and she looked up to see slowly advancing dark grey clouds. They looked like winter clouds. She thought that the weather forecasters had said that it was supposed to be warm this weekend.

Molly watched as the clouds grew thicker and moved a little faster. A sudden clap of thunder startled her as snow began to fall from the dark clouds that were spreading out rapidly over the town.

Chapter Two

By the time Karla got home from work at 5:30, Littletown was in the middle of a snowstorm. The local radio stations began to broadcast cancellations and the forecasters were scrambling for answers.

Molly was reading a manga on the couch and listening to the hard rock radio station when her mother came in, shaking snow off her light jacket in the open doorway.

"It's really coming down!" Karla exclaimed. "There was an accident on Main Street by the post office a little while ago. Your ninth grade English teacher, Tammy Sanders, was rear-ended by some guy."

"Was she hurt?" Molly asked. She hated hearing about car accidents, more so in the last year.

"I don't think so," her mother replied. "She was walking around with the cops checking out the damage to the cars and she didn't go off in an ambulance."

Molly and her mother exchanged a serious glance. Molly wondered if they would finally open up and talk about what happened to her father and how they were *really* doing. It had been a couple of months since they'd said anything about the car accident that had claimed Jack

Parker's life. Brian's vision of seeing him standing beside Molly in the school was still giving her chills. It sure felt like something really crazy was going on – as if reality itself was being shaken.

But Karla didn't want to talk about losing her husband quite yet, and continued on with the topic of the surprise snowstorm.

"The weather forecasters dropped the ball on this one, huh?" she asked her daughter.

"They sure did," Molly said. "I even heard thunder before it started snowing. Pretty freaky, huh?"

"Yeah," her mother replied. "There must be six inches on the ground already! In a couple of hours, we could have a foot!"

For the first time since the snow had started falling, Molly realized the correlation between her dream last night and the snowstorm that was happening now. Had her dream been a premonition?

"How about a nice hot cup of tea?" her mother asked. "I'm feeling better, but I'm beat and a cup of tea sounds like a good way to start the weekend."

"Sure," Molly said. "Who knows, we may get snowed in for the weekend? Maybe we can play some games or something." She got up and followed her mother into the kitchen. She hoped that she could talk about all the odd happenings in the last two days, but was unsure of how to start. With the one year anniversary of the death of her father almost here, it made it all the more difficult.

Karla turned the stove on and filled the kettle from the sink faucet. She took a deep breath and looked at Molly. "It's the decorations around town that drive it home, too," she said, starting to get a little emotional.

She set the kettle on the burner. "It can be so hard to keep in control sometimes."

Molly nodded. She could feel that all-too-familiar lump in her throat again.

Karla got out a couple of teacups and looked out the window at the snow coming down. "I don't know how much you think about it, but these past few days have been pretty rough. It seems like *everything* reminds me of your father..."

"Me, too," Molly agreed.

"Maybe it's time to talk about it," Karla said as evenly as possible. "We've been putting it off long enough."

A few minutes later, they were seated comfortably on the couch in the living room, each with a steaming hot cup of tea.

"I can hardly believe it's been a whole year since the accident," Karla said. "It feels like yesterday, but also like a different life...God, I miss him..."

Molly settled into her mother's arms as she recalled the Halloween of the previous year...

Karla, Molly, and her friends, Candice and Cindy, were sitting on the floor of Molly's apartment, engaged in a competitive game of Monopoly.

"You can't buy *double* hotels!" Molly said to Candice with a look of someone who was just cheated. "I'm going to be there on my next turn. That's not fair!"

Candice picked up her fat wad of colorful bills and fanned herself. "It's just a *game*, Molly," she said in a poor southern accent.

"Whatever," Molly retorted. "You'll be taking a trip to my Boardwalk soon enough!"

"You can take my railroads to get there!" Cindy said, laughing.

"Girls, girls," Karla cut in, raising her hands in a stopping motion. "Take it easy. I'm the banker and I say we let her spend her money."

Candice purchased her hotels and handed the dice to Molly. "Your turn." She pointed to her two hotels on each of the three yellow properties. "Come stay at my hotels. They're real nice!"

Molly shook her head, pushed her glasses up her nose a little, and rolled the dice. She moved her little Scotty dog ahead seven spaces and groaned, "Not again!" She glanced at Candice and stuck out her tongue. "At least I didn't land on your *double hotels*."

Candice waved a hand. "You'll be back."

"Thanks for taking the fabulous Cindy Railroad Express!" Cindy said with a wide smile. "Again." She held out a hand and rubbed her thumb and index finger together. "Pay up, sweetie."

There was knock on the door and Molly turned her head at the sound. She handed Cindy a light brown one-hundred-dollar bill. "That's for your stupid railroad!" she told her friend. "I'll get the door," she added, pushing herself up.

Candice and Cindy sat across from each other on the floor, the Monopoly board on the carpet between them. Karla, sitting opposite her daughter, said, "Remember, just a couple pieces of candy for each trick-or-treater."

"I know," Molly said, rolling her eyes. "You've said it a *hundred* times already."

"Well, remember that we get what's *left*. Maybe your father would like some when he gets home work tonight."

"If Dad was here, he'd have eaten most of it by now," Molly said as she opened the front door.

Her mother laughed, knowing that Jack would have had his fair share by then.

Candice and Cindy reached for the small bowl of candy set aside for the quartet of gamers as Molly flung the door open. They looked on, curious as to what costumes the kids at the door would be wearing. Cindy unwrapped a butterscotch candy and popped it into her mouth. Candice had picked out a piece of peppermint candy, but hesitated to unwrap it as she saw who was standing in the doorway.

"Dad?" Candice asked. "What are you doing here?"

Tony Andrews was wearing his police uniform – not a costume – and he looked like he was about to cry. He swallowed as he looked at Molly and turned his hat nervously in his hands.

"Mind if I come in?" he asked.

Molly stepped aside, still holding the doorknob.

Tony directed his gaze at Karla. "There's been an accident," he said quietly.

The blood drained from Karla's face. "Dear God..." she whispered. "Jack!"

"There's no easy way to say it. No nice way..." Tony said as he stepped inside the apartment.

There was an uneasy stillness in the room as Karla and the three girls all looked at the policeman they knew. There was an air of dread around the man.

Tony began slowly. "A drunk driver collided with Jack's car just outside town, almost a mile out. The driver was going way too fast. Jack didn't have time to react." He shook his head at the inadequacy of his words.

Tears welled up in Karla's eyes and her hands began to shake.

"It's just one of those things," Tony said. "The guy hit Jack head-on and…" He faltered, desperately not wanting to actually say the thing he came to say. "Jack was killed instantly," he finished, as a tear rolled down his cheek.

Molly was still standing with the doorknob in her hand. She looked at her mother, stunned by the news and unable to believe what she had just heard. Candice and Cindy sat quietly, also in disbelief.

"I'm so sorry, Karla! Jack was a good friend," he said as another tear fell, "a good man."

Karla slowly shook her head from side to side as she tried to make sense of what she'd just been told. Molly closed the door in a daze and went to her mother. She dropped into a sitting position and looked at her mother's anguished face as Molly's tears fell.

"Oh, Molly!" Cindy gasped. "I'm so sorry!"

Candice reached out and tenderly put a hand on Molly's arm. Tears flowed freely as she whispered, "Sorry, Molly…"

Molly lay in her mother's arms as they comforted each other.

The tea had cooled some by the time they were ready to talk about the pain from the loss they shared. They agreed that it wouldn't matter if they were home or out. They were hurting, and the anniversary of Jack Parker's deadly accident was impossible to avoid. They discussed options, talked about the things they missed about him, and Molly reminded her mother of the dream she'd had about being out in the snowstorm – which seemed quite uncanny now that a real snowstorm had struck Littletown.

Karla fixed a simple supper and they talked as they ate. They left the radio on and listened as updates about strange weather all over the globe came in. There were tornadoes in the Midwest, huge waves along the Atlantic and Pacific coasts, and earthquakes throughout Central America. Monsoon-like rains stormed across tropical islands, and bitter-cold winds over 100 kilometers per hour blew across much of the land and sea at both the North and South Poles. Outside their own apartment, the snow continued to fall and the wind drove hard.

"I've been having nightmares almost every night since the beginning of the month," Karla said after supper. "I've had them on and off for the last year, but the last few weeks have been wretched." She smiled sadly. "You don't know what you got 'til it's gone, right?"

Molly gave her mother a huge hug. "We still got each other."

"Thanks, Molly Margaret," her mother said gratefully. This time, her tears were less sad.

An hour later, after wishing her daughter good night, Karla was curled up in bed. She had taken Jack's golden pocket watch from the dresser, where he usually had it hung by the side of the mirror, and held it tightly under the covers. It had been something special to him, but Karla had never been told why, or how, he had gotten it. It was one of the few personal items he'd left behind that she treasured. It comforted her. She slept with it often. She cried a little as she thought of him. A short while later, she fell asleep with the golden pocket watch still clutched in her hands…

Karla dreamed. It was night in her dream. Jack was driving his red Toyota sedan. He was pulling out onto a main road. He smiled at the children in their Halloween costumes who were carrying orange bags bulging with candy. He cruised. Karla could make out a dark shape in the night that seemed to be following Jack's car.

She knew that she was dreaming, but she could not wake herself even though she struggled to pull herself away from what she knew would be coming soon...

The dark shape had a human form and seemed to be holding something thin and long, something like a staff. A long piece jutting out at the top of the staff caught her attention – the glint of metal.

Jack drove on, not noticing the dark figure that floated behind his car. The figure grew more defined. Karla recognized the figure now – the black-robed figure of the grim reaper – Death! There was no mistaking the skeletal figure in a black, tattered, flowing robe. Clutched in Death's skeletal hands was a scythe.

Still oblivious to the figure of Death following close behind him, Jack glanced from side to side at the children in their costumes. Death grew larger with each passing moment, looming over the car with his scythe held threateningly over one shoulder.

An oncoming car, with bright headlights, swerved in front of Jack's car and the two vehicles collided violently. Bits of plastic, metal, and glass, scattered over the road.

Death swooped down through the car's hood, swinging his scythe.

"No!" Karla shouted in her dream.

Death slowly rose from the car, holding Jack's limp body under one arm. Jack was not dead yet and he looked at his wife, reaching out to her. But she could not save him from Death. The black-robed figure flew up into the night sky with Jack held firmly to his side, vanishing into the darkness…

Karla woke up from her nightmare with a start. She was still holding Jack's pocket watch, the gold chain gathered in a palm. She reached out from under the covers and flipped on the small lamp beside her bed. Then she set the pocket watch beside the base of the lamp.

"Oh, Jack," she whispered. "I miss you so much…" She cried bitter tears and shook with the pain of grief. One year, and the pain was still as sharp as it had been the night Tony had delivered the terrible news. She cursed the drunk driver, who now sat in some cell for his crime. She hoped he suffered. It did not comfort her, but she wished it all the same.

*

Molly was lying in bed staring at the painting her father had given her for her tenth birthday. She had not seen anything unusual in it since seeing the Centaur the night before. Even though she and her mother had opened up to the tragedy of losing her father, Molly had decided that she

34

would keep the Centaur sighting and Brian's vision (or whatever it was) to herself for now.

Too many odd things were happening, though. Molly felt like something strange, or amazing, was going to happen. Only, she wasn't sure if it was good or not. If the library was open in the morning, she thought she might go down and find a couple books on the paranormal. She didn't trust what she would find on the internet, and dial-up took forever to connect. Maybe the ghost of her father was trying to contact her. It wasn't something that frightened her – she had loved her father dearly and missed him terribly – but it did make her uneasy.

Her clock radio was on the station that played hard rock. It wasn't loud. Between songs, the DJ kept giving updates on the unusual weather. Molly was barely listening as she wondered what all the recent, and strange, occurrences could mean. She also kept looking at the painting, hoping for a glimpse of the Centaur again. She thought about sending Brian an e-mail asking him about what he'd seen in detail, but decided against it. It took too long, for one thing. Also, she wasn't sure how to word it.

She rolled on to her back and looked at the wall that her bed was up against. There was a movie poster, a manga-style drawing of a flying cat that she'd done a few months ago, and the poster of her favorite rock band on that wall. A first place track medal was further down the wall, almost in the corner of the room, by her feet.

The hall clock chimed eleven times. She yawned.

Realizing that she was exhausted, she got up and turned off the radio. She got in bed, flicked the light off, and pulled the covers up to her chin.

She fell asleep thinking about what would happen between her and Brian the next time they met, and not just about him seeing her father.

Molly found herself standing in a snowstorm and wearing the clothes the girl with the red mittens had left her. The canteen and pouch were slung over her left shoulder.

"Nice," Molly said. "Dreaming again…" Even though she was aware of it being a dream, it felt real – just like her dream the night before when she had been standing on the grassy mound with the young girl.

It was as if no time had passed at all since her dream the night before. The mound was gone, the foot of snow lay around her in all directions, and the only light came from the few streetlights that she could see close to her. Everything beyond fifteen yards was swallowed up in the darkness and blowing snow.

"Still sucks," Molly muttered. She shook her head. At least she had boots on in this dream. Nice ones, too.

Molly began to walk through the snow, heading nowhere in particular. She called out a few times, asking if anyone was there. No reply came and she did not see any tracks but her own in the snow. She walked for some time, following the streetlights. The snow was up to her knees and she was tiring when she decided to stop. Feeling thirsty, she took a sip from the canteen. The liquid was sweet. It tasted like a fruit juice concoction, delicious and refreshing. It filled her belly and warmed her cheeks. She capped the canteen and continued to trudge through the snow.

When the snow finally began to let up, it seemed as though hours had passed. Molly was able to see structures around her now that the streetlights were not hampered by the snowstorm. She was on Main Street in Littletown, as if she'd been walking in place for hours. The roads were clear of snow, and traffic. No one was on the sidewalk, and she could not see anyone inside the buildings through the windows facing the street.

As she passed the library, a familiar voice came from the still town.

"Hey, Molly," the voice said in a friendly and easy tone.

Molly turned to find the girl with the red knitted mittens sitting on the front steps of the library. Molly walked over to her and sat down.

"This is my dream. What are you doing here?" Molly asked.

"Just thinking," the young girl replied. She motioned with a hand out toward the street. "What do you see?"

Molly looked at the snow-covered town resting in the darkness around them and shrugged. "I can see the bank...the liquor store...the post office where my mom works." She pointed at it, almost directly across Main Street from where the two of them sat. "And lots of snow. What do *you* see?"

"I see an empty place," the girl stated, as if she'd prepared her response before Molly had even asked the question. "There is no one doing business at the bank. The liquor store has beautiful decorations, yet without anyone to admire them. The post office is vacant as well – no letters being sent, no letters being delivered. A ghost town is what I see."

"Well, it *is* the middle of the night and the snowstorm just ended. But, yeah, everybody's gone," Molly said. "I hadn't thought of it being a ghost town."

The girl stood up and held out a hand. "There is something I want to show you," she said, carrying on as if Molly hadn't spoken.

Molly rolled her eyes. She was getting annoyed at the riddles, but took the girl's hand. After all, it *was* dream, and she was curious.

The girl led Molly out onto Main Street. They stopped in the middle of the road, looking down the street toward Molly's apartment. Suddenly, they were standing in Molly's bedroom. The girl pointed at the painting of Littletown on the wall. Molly gasped, covering her mouth with a hand. Standing in the foreground of the painting was her father! He was smiling broadly, facing out from the painting, with his hands behind his back.

Molly leaned closer. He was just as she remembered him, broad smile, confident, and almost child-like, as though he was proud to be an adult that had held on to his youthful ways. He was clever and fun. It came through so clear that it was more like a photograph than a painting.

"I miss him," Molly said longingly. "I'd do *anything* to see him again!"

"I thought so," said the girl with the red mittens.

"I wish there was some way to go back in time and change things, reverse the accident…" Molly said wistfully, no longer caring that it was just a dream. She felt as though she was saying what she truly felt. "Why was he taken?" she added angrily. "Why couldn't it have been someone else?!"

"There are reasons," the girl replied. "He was in the wrong place at the wrong time. Even the most powerful of us cannot stop the things we do not like."

Molly felt that painful twinge in her guts and that uncomfortable lump in her throat. She was on the verge of tears. "If only there was some way to change that. Make things *right*." As she spoke, her father vanished from the painting. "Why did you show me that?" she asked, upset that she was shown something that hurt. "Is there something I can do?"

"Perhaps," the girl said. "There is someone I know whom you should meet. We may be able to do that *something*."

"Really?" Molly asked, feeling hopeful. Did she dare get her hopes up?

The young girl with the red knitted mittens looked up at Molly with a confident smile and said, "Really."

Sunlight came through the closed curtains in Molly's bedroom. It was bright. Molly blinked and rubbed her eyes. She shoved the covers aside and flung her feet over the side of the bed. She put her glasses on and looked at the painting of Littletown. It had not changed. Her father had not been painted in the foreground.

Only a dream, Molly, she told herself. *A dream of wishful thinking.*

When she went into the kitchen, her mother was reading the Saturday paper at the table. Karla looked better, the red gone from her nose, and her eyes were brighter, clearer.

They wished each other a good morning and Molly sat down at the table opposite her mother. "Roads are closed all over, but the paper got through!" Karla said, shaking the paper a little for emphasis.

Molly nodded, but her mind was elsewhere. "Can I ask you a question?"

Karla folded the paper and set it on the table. "Sounds serious," she said, raising one eyebrow. "What ya got?" she asked.

Molly was still a little sleepy, but she had woken with a sense of hope she'd not had in over a year. "Do you think that we ever get the chance to change things? Like, when we die or something and maybe we can go back and change, I don't know, three important things…three things that changed our lives. Or, maybe just one. One *big* one."

Karla took a sip of coffee and then a bite of toast. She knew what her daughter was getting at. Karla had thought about some crazy things herself in the past year, many of those things dark, and things she'd kept to herself. "That would be quite fantastic," she said, trying to be open. She did not want to shut her daughter down, no matter how wild a theory Molly came up with.

"I don't mean jumping around like some sort of time traveler…Just go back and change one thing," Molly said wistfully. "Like, maybe, stopping an accident before it could happen."

"Life doesn't work that way, honey," Karla said kindly. "Thinking like that can make your mind go in circles. Accepting life and what it is can be difficult, but that's how things work."

"If I could just send a message," Molly said, thinking out loud. "Find a way to warn him, tell him not to drive that night…Maybe he would be here now and none of this would have ever happened…"

Karla set her mug down and took Molly's hands in hers. "You sound like your father. He was always talking about time travel, other dimensions, and other worlds," she said, still speaking kindly. It was good to think of Jack in that way, like a grown up version his child-self, full of imagination and a sense of adventure. "But he's gone, and that's the way it is."

Molly pulled her hands free from her mother's and got up from the table. She looked out the window at the snow-covered town as she got the cereal down. A foot or more had accumulated overnight. Now it was almost two feet deep.

"I can't help thinking the way I do," Molly stated with a touch of anger in her voice. She didn't care if she sounded a little irrational. She refused to believe that life didn't have *some* kind of magic in it. "And I can't stop thinking about Dad."

Karla leaned back in her chair, the memory of her dream from last night still clear in her head. The black-robed figure of Death carrying Jack away from her had been with her since waking. "Me neither," she said slowly, absent-mindedly tapping the edge of her coffee mug with her bare left ring-finger. "Me neither."

Molly turned to face her mother. "I don't care how crazy I sound. If anyone can find a way to change things, it's me."

Chapter Three

The severe snowstorm had practically shut the town down by the time Molly got up (a little after eight) on Saturday morning. It came as no surprise when Candice called to ask what Molly was up to while Molly was eating breakfast. With the many road closures and most places not open for business, it was a perfect excuse to hang out; which meant watching movies, playing games, drinking hot chocolate, snacking, and talking about whatever was new, interesting, or, knowing her friend, boys.

Candice Andrews was Molly's closest friend, even though she was also good friends with Cindy Carter. With permission from the parents of both young women, it was decided that Candice would spend the day at Molly's.

Candice only lived a couple blocks away, on Lee Street. Walking was safer than driving and while the storm was unusually early for that part of the country, Littletown had plenty of snowstorms in the winter and the girls had walked to each other's homes during all kinds of weather. Candice and Cindy hadn't gotten their driver's licenses yet, and Molly, who had only gotten her license a few months ago, didn't drive much.

It was almost eleven that morning by the time Candice arrived. Molly and Candice were sitting in Molly's room listening to the radio and chatting about random items of interest; the storm, classes they liked or despised, new movies, music and books, childhood memories, and, of course, Cindy's recent news.

"Has Cindy called or sent you an e-mail yet today?" Molly asked Candice. "Or, last night?"

Candice shook her head. "No. I heard about Rob at school yesterday between classes, and that was it. She'll be spending all her time with him now."

Molly shrugged. "I can't really be too upset, though. It's not like this is the first time or anything...at least Rob isn't a dork like some of her other guys."

"Or Brian," Candice said teasingly.

"What?" Molly asked, taken off-guard.

"Oh, come on, Mol," Candice said with a wicked grin. "Cindy and I know you like him. He's cute. You look at him sometimes, well, a lot. Of course you like him!"

"Whatever," Molly said, blushing a little.

Candice chuckled at her small victory. "What? Do you think we're blind?" she asked, not wanting to get Molly too riled up, but still enjoying the tease.

Molly was thinking about Brian and what he had said about seeing her father on Friday after school. She glanced over at the painting of Littletown on her wall.

She gasped in surprise.

There, in the foreground, painted in, as if he'd always been there, just like in her dream from the night before, her father stood, looking out of the painting with his broad smile and hands behind his back!

"What is it?" Candice asked, noticing Molly's stark reaction. She looked at where Molly was staring with wide eyes – the painting of Littletown. It didn't look any different to her.

"You didn't see that?" Molly asked her friend. "That thing in the painting?" She could not see her father in it now, but he *had* been there. She was absolutely certain of it.

"Um, no," Candice replied. "It looks like it always does – boring." She meant it to be a joke, but Molly's reaction said that she did not take it that way.

"My dad gave that to me for my birthday a few years ago," Molly said defensively. "It's special to *me*."

Candice sat quietly, remembering how terrible Molly's loss had been. She put a hand on her friend's shoulder. "Are you okay?"

Molly turned away from the painting with her father's image lingering in her mind. "Yeah, I'm alright," she said, trying to play it cool. It had not been a trick of her mind – she'd seen her father in the painting. She had kept the secret of seeing the Centaur in the painting from her mother, and Brian's vision as well. She was going to do her best to keep this incident a secret, too. She changed the subject, hoping Candice would forget about it. "I've got a question for ya," Molly said, tucking her hair behind her ears.

"What?" Candice asked, hoping that she hadn't hurt her friend's feelings too bad.

44

"Do you think that it's possible to get a second chance?" Molly asked.

"What do you mean?" Candice probed. "Like…re-taking a test? Or your mom dating?"

Molly had wondered about her mother dating, but it didn't seem likely in the near future. She decided to be direct with her friend. "We watch movies about time travel and alternate worlds and different realities. Read about them, too. Do you think that those things are possible? Maybe my dad is alive in another reality, or maybe I could send a message back in time to warn him about the drunk driver…"

"I don't think so," Candice said slowly. "That's just in the movies and books." She did not want to upset Molly anymore. She'd been there when her father had told Molly and Karla that Jack had been killed. A year was a long time, but not *that* long. They all remembered it well.

Molly shrugged and glanced back at the painting. "Yeah. It's just something I've been thinking about lately. I miss him. I guess I think that people don't always make things up. Maybe people who *believe* that they can time travel *actually can*. Maybe people who think they can move things with their mind *actually can*. But as soon as they stop thinking that they can, they *lose* that power. Maybe there *is* a wardrobe that leads to another world, or there *is* a machine that can travel through time. Art reflects life, right?"

Candice couldn't tell if her friend was joking or not. Molly sounded serious, and they had talked about stuff like this before – but not in a way where Molly was directly relating it to her dead father. She wasn't sure how to respond. Luckily, Molly continued before she said anything.

"I can't believe it's been a year already," Molly said, lost in thought.

"There are days when I wake up and think I'll see him sitting at the table for breakfast." She paused.

"My dad says that kind of thing is normal," Candice said. "He has all these books on stuff like that. You know, his brother was killed when he was only ten. He says that he still sees him sometimes – in his mind."

"Yeah, your dad is cool about those things," said Molly. She was looking at the painting, wondering if her father would reappear again. The Centaur had only been there once. While her father had appeared in it twice, the first time had been in her dream. What would show up next?

There was a moment where both young women didn't speak, the music on the radio the only sound in the room.

"I heard that a new family is going to move to town," Candice said to change the subject. "My mom said that they hired this new guy from Salt Lake City, or someplace out west, to work on this new project they are doing in the lab."

"Yeah?" Molly asked. "What are they working on?"

"I don't know," Candice replied. "Boring stuff probably, but they have a son who's about our age," Candice said with a knowing smile. "His name's David Carson."

"Oh," Molly said, turning away from the painting. Her friend didn't always relay information correctly. Still, something about the name 'David Carson' piqued her interest. It was as if she'd heard his name before, or knew someone else by that name. "You think your mom is going to hook you up?" she asked, taking the opportunity to tease her friend.

Candice grinned. They were back on good terms again and talking about stuff Candice felt more comfortable with. "Did you see that 'sold' sign across the street a couple days ago?"

"No," Molly admitted. "Someone bought that place?"

"Hello, Molly!" Candice said sarcastically. "The Carsons bought it. David is going to live across the street from you!"

"Really?" Molly asked, still feeling like David Carson was a familiar name she knew but couldn't place.

Candice nodded.

There was a light knock on the door and Karla opened the door enough to peek her head into the room. "Lunch is ready, if you are."

Candice looked at Molly and nodded. "I'm hungry."

"OK, Mom," Molly said, getting off the bed. She took one last look at the painting before heading out to the kitchen.

They spent the day playing games, watching a movie, listening to music and chatting – although not about Molly's father anymore. It snowed the entire time, although not as heavily. The wind blew hard and cold, causing creaks and pops in the walls. After supper, the two teens sat down at the table to play a game of Boggle with Karla.

Candice left after a couple of games. She called from home a few minutes later to tell Molly that she'd made it without being buried, frozen, or blown away, and that the snow was above her waist in some spots.

After wishing her mother a good night, Molly went into her room to draw. With it being a Saturday night, the oldies music program was on and Molly enjoyed listening to the hits from the '50's and '60's. She sat at her desk, turning the lamp on and leaving the overhead light off. It set a better mood, made it feel calmer. With pencil in hand, she drew the first thing that came to her mind: the path that went through Littletown. It had been part of the railroad decades ago, but that train didn't run anymore and it was a nice trail that went by Littletown Lake. Molly liked the way the overhanging trees made it look like a tunnel in the summer. She drew until almost eleven, until she could barely keep her eyes open.

She could hear the wind as it blew against her window. The snow was almost up to the windowsill. Molly crawled into bed and gave one last look at the painting on the wall. After seeing her father in it that morning, nothing else had appeared. She let out a disappointed, "Hm," and then pulled the covers up to her nose. She fell asleep quickly, wondering what she would dream about that night…

Molly began to dream as soon as she was asleep. She was standing on the path beside the Crest River. It was summer. The river meandered lazily through landscape. The air was warm and dozens of different insects buzzed around her. Birds were singing. Light, fluffy clouds drifted slowly above. The path that led out to the lake ran beside the river. Molly knew the trail well. It was the one she'd been drawing before she'd gone to bed. She'd jogged the trail countless times in preparation for her long-distance runs with the track team. She loved to run outdoors. It made her feel free.

"Now this dream *doesn't* suck," Molly said with a genuine smile.

Molly began to walk beside the river, watching as the flowing water rippled along its course. As she approached the bridge that crossed the river, she noticed the girl with the red mittens sitting on the far side of it.

"Hey, Molly," the girl said in a friendly greeting.

"Hey, you," Molly returned. "How come you keep showing up in my dreams?"

"There is someone I would like you to meet," the young girl said, ignoring Molly's question. "He may be able to help you – or, you may be able to help us."

Molly stopped walking and looked down at the girl. The girl was still wearing the same clothing; bundled up for cold weather. The girl's long bangs were still partially covering her eyes. Although now, in the sunlight, Molly could see the girl's eyes a little better. They were strange. There was very little white, most of her eyes were black, as if nearly all pupil. Not scary, but definitely odd.

The air grew heavy. Molly felt as if she were moving under water. The birds stopped singing and the insects were silent. Molly slowly turned her head. The water had stopped flowing in the Crest River and the land around her was still, with no breeze at all. She looked down to ask the girl what was going on, but the girl was no longer by her side.

An old man in a white robe strode forward. He stood in front of Molly and looked her over with keen, light blue eyes. His white beard covered his mouth and fell down below his knees. A golden belt was tied around his waist. "So," he said in a calm voice, "we meet at last."

Molly raised an eyebrow and put her hands on her hips. "And you are…?"

"Why, I am Father Time!" the old man said with a kind smile. (His beard moved slightly and Molly assumed it was a smile under the full beard.) Father Time's eyes sparkled as he looked at her kindly, but also with an appraising look, as though he was sizing her up. "I have been informed that you would do…almost *anything* to have your father with you again," he added in a very mysterious manner. He leaned toward her, both hands wrapped around his long staff that was planted on the ground.

Molly nodded, "Yeah…" she said, wondering where this was going. Again, she knew that she was dreaming but this felt *real*.

Father Time nodded. "Hmm…Walk with me," he said, gesturing with a hand down the path.

Curious, Molly stepped up beside him and found that she felt safe and comfortable in his presence. The pressure around her seemed to lift and she could move normally again.

"And what conclusion have you come to?" Father Time asked as they walked.

Molly glanced up at his face. It looked both old and young. The long white beard and wrinkles in his skin did not match his wise and youthful eyes. She was not surprised. He looked kind of like she expected Father Time should. Was it her dream, or his? Or was it that girl's? Did it matter?

"I miss him," Molly said softly. "I don't know, maybe I feel like it was never *supposed* to happen. That it was *wrong…*" she paused, walking slower, and her voice grew passionate. "I don't *want* to accept it. There *has* to be a way to change things! Magic is real," she said. "Maybe not in wands or fairy dust, but it's out there!"

Father Time laughed a little.

"I'm serious!" Molly said defensively. "I believe in magic."

Father Time stopped walking and stood with the sun over his

shoulder. "I only laugh because it is a rare World where the natives with intelligence do *not* believe in magic. What are emotions, feelings, or even life itself, if not magic?" he asked.

Molly squinted in the sun's direct light. With the light beside his head, Father Time looked almost magical himself. "Like, fear and hate are magic?" she asked, not quite sure about how *they* could be magic.

Father Time nodded. "What one can imagine…flying machines, radios, music, and art, are forms of magic. But I did not come to explain this to you. I came to meet you, to see who you truly are. Here, in this dream, nothing is hidden from me. I can see the love you have for your father, and the passion in your words is as true inside you."

"There's a hole inside, too," Molly said sadly, holding a fist over her heart. "It has been there since my father died."

Father Time took a deep breath and looked at her calmly. "People die, Molly. That is the way of it. It simply happens."

"For some," Molly said evenly. "But with all these weird things going on, I believe more than ever that something magical is happening and I am going to figure it out. I am *not* giving up."

Father Time bent down a little. He was almost a foot taller than her and they were eye to eye when he asked, "Do you believe that you can be reunited with your father?"

Molly nodded without hesitation. "Absolutely," she said with one, firm nod.

Father Time straightened and smiled – again, it was the movement of his beard. "Good. We will discuss this more the next time we meet."

"So, it went well?"

Molly looked down and saw the girl with the red mittens standing beside them. She had not seen the girl arrive. "I guess so," Molly replied, not sure of what was really going on.

"Excellent," the girl said. "Time to get going."

Molly's eyes fluttered open. She could hear her mother showering and humming "Monster Mash" in the shower. It was good to hear her mother sounding so happy. Something was changing in her mother. Molly was sure that it had something to do with all the odd things going on in the last few days. She grinned, feeling like her life was finally about to get better. Her mother's humming reminded her that today was Halloween.

Molly got out of bed, put her glasses on, and was mildly surprised to see her father back in the painting again. Her grin grew wider. She took a step closer to it. He was still there, as if he'd been painted in it from the beginning. She took another step and reached out to touch her father's image. The paint was dry.

What's going on? she thought. *This is real! I'm not imagining this! He's there – in the painting!* She leaned forward so that she was just a few inches from the paint. "What's happening?" she whispered to the painting.

Her father didn't move or answer, just stood smiling with his hands behind his back.

The water stopped running in the bathroom and she could still hear her mother humming. It sounded like an Enya song.

Molly stepped back from the painting, wondering if she should run to the bathroom, pound on the door, and demand that her mother come right away to see this appearance in the painting. But maybe the reason all these things seemed to be happening to her alone meant that these things were just for her and no one else.

Her father's image faded a moment later when the bathroom door opened. Two seconds later, he was gone.

"Figures," Molly said.

It's a sign, she thought to herself. *It has to mean something...that something is going to happen soon!*

Molly went out to the kitchen and poured herself a cup of coffee. She poured a healthy amount of Irish creamer into it and looked out the window. The snow was still falling and it looked like three feet was on the ground now. She felt like this was all happening for a reason, that the whole world was telling her that she was right. There was magic in the world, and it was growing stronger. She could not hold it in any longer. She started talking quickly as soon as her mother came out to the kitchen.

"I had another dream last night," Molly said excitedly. "Father Time was in it. The girl with the red mittens was in it, too. I know it's the same girl I saw when I was getting my hair done at Sandra's. She's been trying to show me things in my dreams. Just like the stuff that Dad used to talk about. I've been seeing things in the painting that Dad got me for my birthday a few years ago, for my tenth birthday. I saw a Centaur in it: and Dad – twice! I think that's why he gave it to me...like, its magic or something. And Brian said he saw Dad standing beside me at school on Friday. I think all these strange things are happening because something big is happening. No, not big...like, huge!"

Karla had not been expecting such a barrage first thing on a Sunday morning and she stood looking at her daughter with a confused expression for a moment.

"The dream last night was just like the last two. It was like the dreams lasted all night long...but, the dreams *weren't* that long," Molly continued, undaunted by her mother's expression. "And they are *real*. Not just something in my imagination while I'm sleeping. No, these dreams are like I am *there!* It's a real place. As real as this apartment! Have you ever had dreams like that?"

Karla was still grappling with the avalanche of words and the meaning behind them. She refilled her coffee mug and said, "I really don't know." She was thinking of her vivid dream about losing Jack to Death. The theme was something she'd dreamed about for a whole year. "They can be pretty intense. We don't know a lot about why we dream," she added. It was uncanny how much Molly was like her father – more so now than ever before. But was that such a bad thing? She had not seen Molly this alive since the heartbreaking news they had received one year ago.

"Well, it's Halloween. I just know that something is going to happen today. Something amazing!" Molly said, certain that whatever it was she was going to be ready.

Karla was a little worried that her daughter might be taking her dreams too far, but she had also felt like something mysterious was happening. Not to the extent that her daughter was, but she could not deny that she felt happier. And she'd had a dream about Jack last night that was not like the others she'd been having. Not like the one where Death took Jack away from her. It had been a happy dream, where she was reunited with him and they had been on the trail that went to the lake. That was all she could recall, but the good feeling had followed her into the waking world. She felt happy, something she hadn't expected on the one year anniversary of Jack's fatal accident.

Karla and Molly laughed and smiled more than usual over breakfast. Karla could feel the extraordinary changes in her daughter and herself growing. It was a welcome change, and one that she knew her daughter was setting in motion.

Molly was in a good mood all day. She looked at the painting a few dozen times, but it was just the one of the town without a mythical being or her father reappearing. She drew, watched the snowstorm, and tried to do some homework. She talked on the phone with Candice for a bit and sent Cindy an e-mail. Mostly about the weather and that school would probably be canceled on Monday, but also about her thoughts on how she felt like something amazing was going to happen that day.

At supper, Molly was a little less excited, and wondering if she had missed the big thing that she knew would happen. She also considered that it might not happen until she was asleep, and dreaming.

To pass the time, Karla and Molly sat at the kitchen table with mugs of hot chocolate and bowls of popcorn as they played a game of cribbage. Karla dealt the first hand. Molly picked up her cards, slowly separating them to reveal one card at a time. She had the five of clubs, seven of hearts, jack of hearts, five of diamonds, five of spades, and the eight of hearts. Molly's heart skipped a beat.

"What?" her mother asked with a questioning grin.

Molly shook her head and did a poor job of suppressing her smile.

She plucked the seven and eight from her hand and slid them face down on the table for her mother's crib.

This is it! This could be the sign you've been waiting for!

Molly remembered her father explaining the rules of cribbage to her years ago. He'd said, "In cribbage, there's something called a 'perfect hand.' It consists of three fives and a jack. If a five with the same suit as the jack in your hand is cut from the deck, then you have one. No hand has more points – twenty-nine points are the highest a player can score in one hand."

Molly cut the deck. Her mother picked up the top card, flipped it over, and set it on top of the deck. It was the five of hearts. Molly had a perfect hand! In all the years that they had played she had never had a perfect hand. She almost blurted it out, but wanted to play it out.

"Ten," she said, putting down the jack of hearts.

Her mother set down the jack of diamonds. "Twenty, for two." She moved one of her pegs two spaces on the cribbage board.

Molly set down a five. "Twenty-five."

"Go," her mother said, not having a card under a six.

Molly set down another five. "Thirty for two…and last card makes three." She moved her peg ahead three spaces.

Karla looked at the cards lying on the table. She looked at her daughter. She turned her cards on the table face down and played a queen. "Ten."

Molly couldn't help the wide smile on her face, or spreading her arms out wide after she played her last five and said, "Fifteen for two!" She had not flipped her cards over on the table and Karla was looking at them with a surprised smile.

"A perfect hand!" her mother exclaimed.

Molly organized her four cards so they were spread out, but still touching. "Twenty-nine sweet points," she said smugly, running her hands through her hair. She tucked it behind her ears and tilted her chin up in triumph. "I told you something was going to-"

A loud knock came from the front door that startled both Molly and her mother. They looked at each other for a second, Molly's eyes even wider than Karla's. The knock came again. Molly bolted to her feet and headed into the living room. She reached the front door and hesitated a moment, her mind racing wildly at who it could be. Would her father be standing there? What would she do if he was? She flipped the outside light on.

She took hold of the doorknob and took a deep breath. Her whole body was tingling and she could smell that same strange smell she's noticed at Sandra's a few days ago. Kind of like something electrical burning.

She flung the door open.

It was dark outside. No one was standing there. Her heart sank a little.

"Who is it?" her mother asked, walking up behind her.

The walkway had been shoveled recently and only an inch or two of snow was covering the area beyond the front door and up to the sidewalk. However, Molly didn't see any footprints. It reminded her a little of the first dream she'd had with the girl wearing red mittens.

"No one," Molly replied, confused. "Maybe it's a prank." She doubted that the neighbors would do it. They were quiet neighbors for the most part.

"Then close the door, the cold is coming in."

Molly looked at the mounds of snow all around. Some of the snowdrifts were six feet high. There was no traffic and no one on the sidewalks. The thought of it being a ghost town seemed plausible right then. She caught sight of a small package sunk deep in the snow a few feet to her right, mostly buried in the drift to the side of the apartment. It was poorly wrapped with a hand-written tag that read, "To: Molly." She picked it up. It was a box about three inches high, three inches wide, and three inches deep. It had small bow on top. The bow was what had caught her attention. She took it inside and closed the door.

"What do you think it is?" she asked her mother as they went back into the kitchen.

Karla shrugged and asked, "What does it say on the tag?"

"It says it's to me," Molly replied as they sat down at the kitchen table.

"Well, are you going to open it?" her mother asked, almost as curious to see what was in it as Molly was.

Molly ripped the gift open. It was a little black jewelry box with gold trim where the two pieces met. She slowly opened it.

Out of the box she pulled a golden pocket watch on a gold chain. It was the kind of pocket watch with a lid that had to be opened to see the watch face. The watch appeared to be brand new, shining brilliantly under the kitchen light. There was a beautiful carving of a train on the watch lid. Molly didn't know a lot about pocket watches, but she knew that most were molds and not carvings. She trailed her fingers over the golden disc gently. She turned it over in her hands.

"It looks just like your father's," Karla said in awe. "If his wasn't in

58

my room right now, I'd think that someone had taken it and wrapped it up for you."

Molly pressed down on the button at the top of the watch with her thumb. It popped open to reveal the watch face. It was white with black markings and thin black hands. There was a photo on the inside of the lid. Molly's eyes began to water.

"What is it?" her mother asked in concern.

Molly handed the open watch to her mother as a tear fell down her cheek. It was not what she had been expecting. This was not the miracle she'd hoped for.

Karla took the pocket watch and looked at the picture inside the lid. On it was a picture of Karla, Jack, and Molly, taken shortly before Jack's untimely death. "How...?" Karla asked. She looked up at her daughter. "Who would do this?"

Molly shook her head, mystified and confused. It was not the kind of magic she'd been hoping for. This was simply a reminder of what she and her mother had lost.

Her mother handed the pocket watch back.

Molly took it and saw that the time was correct – six o'clock – but the hands weren't moving. She wound it, spinning the small knob at the top with her index finger and thumb.

"I remember that day," Molly said, looking at the picture. "That was at the end of last summer, the day we went out to the lake for a picnic. Right before..." she didn't finish the sentence. She still believed that something magical could happen, but at a loss as to what it could be. "No one took a picture of us," she stated. "Not that I can remember."

Karla got up and went into her bedroom. She came back with Jack's pocket watch. She sat down and held the watch out beside the one Molly had just received. They were practically identical. The only differences were that Jack's pocket watch had an older picture of just Karla and Jack, and had his initials on the back – "J.D.P"

Molly was beginning to wonder if the watch was just a sign, that maybe there was more to come. That idea made her a little less upset about getting the watch, and even more curious. Maybe it meant something that she had to figure out on her own. Maybe she had to put her initials on hers, or maybe the picture meant something. But, as she thought about those things, she didn't think they were right.

"I think this is a gift from Father Time," Molly said, pursing her lips and thinking aloud. Her forehead was wrinkled as she thought about what the watch could mean, "Maybe I can time travel with it…"

Karla didn't know what to say to that.

Molly liked the way the golden pocket watch felt in her hands. It felt like there could be something magical about it. However, if it *could* let her travel in time, she didn't know because it had not come with any instructions. She set it at different times and waited hopefully. But she remained in her apartment with her mother every time. The snowstorm still raged outside and the clocks in the apartment marched on, one second at a time.

Nothing out of the ordinary happened in the next few hours. They heard over the radio that school was canceled for Monday. With no further knocks on the door, no phantom images of Jack Parker appearing, nor receiving any more mysterious gifts, Karla and Molly wished each other a good night and headed to their bedrooms; Molly with her new pocket watch, and Karla with Jack's. Molly said, "Sweet dreams," with a playful wink and went to bed wondering what would happen next.

Chapter Four

Karla sat on her bed with her knees drawn up to her chin. She was doing her best to remain calm but the strange arrival of Molly's pocket watch, her recent dreams, and the uneasy feeling that something wasn't quite right in the world, had her anxious, even if it wasn't in a bad way. She thought about that Halloween night last year, after Tony had left with Candice and Cindy. She had sat with her daughter, holding her, and shed tears of grief. It had been a long night. Time had passed strangely. Funeral arrangements and calls had been made over the following days. Sympathy cards had arrived in the mail. Eventually, it sank in – her husband was gone, and he wasn't coming back.

Through the haze, she could remember the funeral clearly. It was a closed casket of polished oak, simple, yet fine. It had been a cool day in early November, and it seemed as though the minister had carried on for hours. Thanksgiving had been rough, as had Christmas and bringing in the New Year. But she had managed. Somehow, she had found a way to carry on, as had Molly. In some ways it had brought her closer to her daughter, and in other ways it had left them broken in a way that seemed as though they would never fully heal. Karla's parents had tried to help, but she had never been very close to them and Jack's death changed little in the relationship she had with them. Her friends had been helpful, especially Tony and Elizabeth Andrews. Elizabeth was like a sister to her and Candice like a daughter.

"A year," Karla whispered.

She reached out and picked up Jack's pocket watch. She wasn't sure what to make of it. Perhaps something supernatural *was* going on. The uncanny resemblance of Molly's watch to Jack's was enough to make the hairs on the back of her neck stand up. Had Jack's comments over the years not just been fancy tales, but actually true? Were there other Worlds beyond ours? Were there really Realms where things beyond imagination existed? Did she dare to believe, as Molly did, that Jack wasn't gone forever?

Halloween was the day before All Saints Day – a time when the dead could draw closer to the living than at any other time of the year. Was Jack trying to reach her and Molly during this unique time?

She popped open the watch and looked at the picture of her and Jack that was inside the lid. They were young in the photo. Molly hadn't been born yet. In fact, it looked about the time when Molly had been conceived. In the picture, Karla was wearing a silver necklace with an odd, but beautiful, slender blue gem set in the center of a delicate silver butterfly. The wings spreading out from it were thin and finely detailed. Jack had given the necklace to her on their first wedding anniversary. Karla remembered it fondly, and she still wore the necklace from time to time. In the small photo, she was wearing a sweater that had been damaged and thrown away before Molly was born, making it easy to place when the picture had been taken. Or, supposedly taken: since she didn't remember posing for it. When she'd asked Jack about it all those years ago, he had simply told her that it was something that he had done for himself.

"One year," she said a little louder.

She wanted answers, but her head hurt – *her heart hurt* – and she was tired. More than tired, she was mentally, physically, and spiritually exhausted. Not sure of what the morning would bring, Karla turned off the light and clutched the watch tightly as she drifted into an uneasy sleep...

Karla dreamed that she was walking on the trail that led out to the lake. It was a sunny day. She was holding something in her hand. She looked down and was not surprised to find herself carrying a wicker picnic basket with a red handkerchief laid across it.

Molly came running out in front of her, twirling in a white dress with yellow flowers. Jack ran after his daughter and Molly let out cries of childlike glee as he picked her up and spun her around. She was only eight years old, and Jack lifted her easily in his strong arms.

They walked together for a short while, carefree. Karla's heart was light, happy.

They stopped for a picnic underneath a massive oak tree. Karla leaned back against the tree trunk as they ate. It was peaceful. She was content and full of love.

It was a good dream, similar to the one she'd had the night before.

After the meal, they continued down the path toward the lake. Jack walked arm-in-arm with Karla. He held Molly's hand as she walked beside him, on his left.

"The two most beautiful women in the land!" he shouted. "To the end of the path – *and beyond!*"

In her dream, her husband's outbursts seemed logical. Every step was full of contentment, and every breath was an intake of joy. She did not want the dream to end.

They passed by an old building that looked familiar to her – very much like the house in which she'd grown up. She felt the urge to go look around inside. "Look!" she said, pointing to it.

Jack and Molly stopped as if reading her mind. They headed over to it and walked inside without a word. The entrance to the house was empty: no furniture or people, other than the Parker family. Not even curtain rods or carpeting. It *was* the house she'd grown up in. Leaving her husband and daughter in the empty living room, she went upstairs to check out her old bedroom. There was something lying on the floor in the far corner by an open window. She went over and bent down to pick it up.

It was a bright red paper heart. She took it and left the room. Jack and Molly had gone back outside. Karla joined them, holding up the paper heart and said, "And beyond!"

They returned to the path and continued to walk until they reached the lake. However, the path no longer ran beside the lake, but straight into it! She could see the lake bottom under the water for about twenty feet out, until it was lost in the murky water. There was thick, green grass on either side of the underwater path.

"Is this the end?" Molly asked, sounding very disappointed.

"Do you *want* to keep going?" her father asked.

Molly did not hesitate. Her dreamy gray eyes were wide with excitement, and they said the thing she did not need to say aloud – she would keep going for as long as she could. Molly headed for the lake, pulling her father with her, and Karla, still locking arms with Jack, went along, unafraid.

As soon as her head was underwater, Karla's found that she could breathe. Instead of feeling as if she was in water, she felt as though the water around her was lighter than the air had been above the water. She could also see the underwater scenery around her very clearly. It was beautiful. Everything was a light shade of green or blue, with the sunlight casting sparkling rays through the water from above. The underwater plants swayed hypnotically back and forth as if in a slow current.

It was serene. Karla was at peace. It was a good dream.

Chapter Five

Molly held her new gold pocket watch as she sat hunched forward on her bed, running her fingers across the small crevices that formed the image of a train on the front. It was mostly the engine, but she could see a couple of the cars behind it. There was smoke billowing out of the engine's smokestack. She could also see a little bit of the track in the foreground. She'd seen her father's pocket watch before, but she'd never really *looked* at it.

She glanced up at the painting of Littletown, curious to see if the Centaur or her father would pop into the foreground. Neither did.

Molly let out a strange sound, a combination of a laugh and a snort. It made her giggle a little. Her heart was beating a little faster tonight, but not in fear or confusion. She was excited. She still felt that something extraordinary was about to happen – and maybe, just maybe, she could change the way things were: make her family whole again.

That feeling she had gotten in her dreams, where she felt more alive, more real, seemed to point at something she couldn't quite figure out. But whatever it was, it was important. She felt as though the last year of her life had been a sort of dream, a bad dream that she'd not been able to wake up from – until a few days ago. It had started when she'd seen the girl with red mittens while she'd been at Sandra's. Then, the Centaur had appeared in her painting…the painting that seemed like a bridge to her father. Was that it? Was he trapped in some weird dimension in the painting? She didn't think so. But the painting *did* have something magical about it now. For over six years it had simply been a gift (that had become a memento) that had hung in her bedroom. But now it felt like an alarm clock that was waking her from this bad dream.

She was anticipating her dream tonight; a dream where, perhaps, Father Time would tell her that her father's death hadn't happened at all. And because she believed they could be reunited, she would wake up and it would be as if the accident had never happened. But that also didn't feel right. The watch she held felt like more than a sign. It felt like a special gift, one with responsibility. As much as she hurt inside, the last year *had* happened. But now, hope had returned. It was a fragile hope and something she wanted to protect.

"I'm going to get an answer tonight," Molly said to the watch. "It's Halloween, but are there any ghosts out tonight?"

She turned to face the window and looked out at the blizzard that was burying the town in snow. It was up to the windowsill, and would block her view before long if it continued to accumulate. Wind was whipping around, playing with the trees and telephone wires. No one was outside. She thought of the dream she'd had when the girl had asked her what she'd seen in the empty town. *A ghost town…*

"No ghosts tonight," Molly repeated, and closed her curtains.

She crawled under the covers, wrapped the gold chain around her knuckles, and held the watch to her heart. She flipped off the light. The night closed in around her. She could feel the faint clicking of the second hand through her fingers as she lay quietly in bed waiting for sleep. Almost as if by sheer will, she fell asleep in a matter of a few seconds.

She was back in the dream.

This one was different, though. She wasn't in Littletown. Molly was standing in a desert. It was late dusk and the sun was hidden from view. There was no vegetation, nor any animals. She was still holding the pocket watch, the chain wrapped around her hand. She looked down at it. When she looked back up, the girl with the red mittens was standing in front of her.

"Subtle," Molly said flatly.

The girl ignored Molly's sarcasm.

"Do you ever take the mittens off?" Molly added in the same flat tone.

The girl looked slightly agitated at that comment and, for a second, Molly thought the girl was going to lose her composure and say something cutting in response. Instead, the girl put on her big smile and said, "Yes, Molly, I do." She gestured to the watch in Molly's hands. "You got it."

"Yep."

The girl tilted her head sideways. "Do you know what it is?"

"I think it's a sign," Molly replied, wondering why Father Time was nowhere in sight. Still, that feeling of excitement was with her and the girl's oddness wasn't going to deter her from figuring out what was going on. "Something that Father Time might use to turn back time."

The girl nodded and looked thoughtful. "I can see how you could come to that conclusion."

"If you know what it is, just tell me!" Molly said, tired of the guessing games.

"That's not how I do things," the girl replied with her big smile. "I will let Father Time do the explaining." She reached out and took Molly's hand in her red mitten.

Suddenly, Molly heard what sounded like thunder coming from all around her. And then it stopped, as suddenly as it had started. The girl let go of Molly's hand.

They were in a darkened room without windows. Father Time sat hunched over in the only chair in the room, looking down at something he held in his hands. The small room smelled dusty and of the earth, as if they were underground. There was no light source, although Molly could see. She tucked her hair behind her ears and noticed that her glasses were gone, even though she could still see clearly. The place felt so ancient that Molly sensed that it had been around since the beginning of time. It was a strange feeling, a little uncomfortable.

"What is it?" Molly asked, taking a couple of steps to stand beside Father Time.

He made no effort to conceal what he was holding as Molly peered over his shoulder. It was a sphere, slightly larger than a softball. There didn't appear to be anything special about the cloudy glass sphere, but Father Time was gazing at it intently as though he saw something in it.

"It is a window into the Worlds and Realms," he said, still gazing at it. He smiled and turned to look at Molly with eyes so intense that Molly was startled by the power behind them. The raw energy coming from Father Time had not been there in her previous dreams. Now, he looked like more than just an old man with youthful eyes. He looked like a god. "It is also a weapon," Father Time explained. "However, one must have the gift of 'other-worldly sight' to use it, and there are few with that power." He glanced at the pocket watch still wrapped around her hand and his smile turned into a look of cautious satisfaction.

Molly held up the watch. It dangled a few inches from her knuckles. "What does it do?" she asked. "I tried turning the knob and winding it, but nothing happened. Can it turn back time?"

Father Time shook his head and stood up, tucking the crystal sphere under an arm and using his staff to push himself up. "Not in the usual sense," he replied. "Different Worlds and Realms have various... consistencies of time. This makes it possible for you to stay consistent in your own...way," he finished, not sounding as sure about it as Molly had hoped. "It has another purpose. A special purpose," he added, sounding far more certain.

"So, what does it do?" she asked again.

Father Time's beard moved slightly upward, indicating a smile. "I will explain in a moment. First, let me welcome you to the Realm of Timeless Wisdom," he said.

Molly was not impressed. "This box of a room is a Realm?" she asked.

"The Realm of Timeless Wisdom is vast," Father Time continued. "This room is a place where I will not be interrupted. There are many

Worlds and Realms. Earth is one of billions of Worlds, many with intelligent life, as the Realm of Timeless Wisdom is one of many Realms – though this Realm could fit many Earths inside it. If one could change the matter to be compatible, that is." He paused for a moment to glance at the young girl behind Molly. "You have been here before, but not to the extent that you are now." He looked back at Molly. "The pocket watch allows you to enter this Realm fully – completely. *This* dream is *real*: as real as anything ever was, or will be. I believe they call it 'astral projection' in your World. You can Travel to every World and every Realm in creation with that device, leaving you unaffected. You are from a World and it is more difficult for those from Worlds to Travel than it is for those from Realms."

Molly nodded. She didn't fully understand everything Father Time said, although she knew a little about astral projection – the ability for the spirit to leave the body – and she was still preoccupied with how all of this would reunite her with her father. Was she going to some kind of afterlife place to get him?

"Now that I'm here," she said carefully, "how does it help me get Dad back?"

Father Time took a deep breath and let it out in a huff as he once again glanced at the young girl behind Molly. "It is more complicated than that. We have a proposition or you."

Molly raised her right eyebrow. "There's a catch? Shocker."

"Mother Nature has gone missing," Father Time said slowly. "This is not a small thing. There has never before been a time when a Keeper has simply…disappeared. Mother Nature's absence is a potentially…

dangerous thing and I have been looking for someone who is determined enough to go and find her. Someone who will not give up. Someone who has the inner strength to overcome the greatest obstacles."

Molly's cheeks flushed. Dream or not, it seemed to her like they had chosen her for some kind of major quest. What were they expecting from her? "Do I have some kind of super powers or something?" she asked.

Father Time nodded. His smile, still an impression through his thick white beard, was genuine and his powerful eyes sparkled with acknowledgement. "Oh, you are something special," he replied with sincere admiration. "You have opened yourself up to *possibilities*. You *believe* in what most consider impossible! That is an *extraordinary* power. You are a dreamer – one who creates for others what they cannot even fathom for themselves!"

Molly had not been expecting that. Father Time's words made her feel absolutely amazing about herself and who she was. No one had ever told her she was special because she liked to think outside the box. Well, her mother and father had said she was special, but in a loving way that parents do to a child. Her father had also encouraged her to be creative and imaginative. But this was Father Time – some kind of *super-being* – who was telling her that she had been the one chosen from the billions of Worlds and Realms because she believed in what other people didn't.

"Cool," she said, not sure of how to respond to his praise. "Thanks."

Father Time nodded. "You are most welcome, my dear." He grew a little more serious and a grave look crossed his wrinkled face. "Mother Nature is a part of us all," he said. "I know your World is feeling the effects of her disappearance already."

73

"The blizzard!" Molly interjected.

"Yes," Father Time agreed. "And this is just the beginning. If this were to continue for an extended period of time, the effects could undo much of creation."

"And this is how I get Dad?" Molly asked, still confused about that part. "Finding Mother Nature will bring him back?"

Father Time shook his head. "No. I will place you back in time one year so that you can prevent his death from ever taking place. I can do more than just allow time to exist, Molly. However, it is a rare thing to allow one to go back in time. But we are desperate and time is growing short. I am a Keeper, like Mother Nature, and it is our duty to help maintain this existence. The Keepers, other than the Dream Keeper from time to time, do not undertake tasks of this kind. We are Keepers after all, not Rescuers, or Finders. And Mother Nature will need a new crystal sphere." He held up the cloudy sphere he had tucked under his arm. "Without it, she cannot maintain control and see where she is needed. It is clear to us that whatever has happened to her, the crystal sphere she had is no longer functioning properly. The Creator has nullified its power and transferred that power to this one. It will activate the moment Mother Nature touches it. But first you must get it to her."

"Alright," Molly replied. "I'm your hero," she added, intending it to be a joke. However, it came out as a statement of fact. She was certain that this wasn't just a dream anymore and the longer she was here, the more real it felt. "So, what's all this about Keepers? Who are you guys? How many of you are there?"

As if on cue, a frightening figure suddenly popped into the small room right beside Father Time. Molly jumped, startled by the sudden appearance. The hooded figure was in black tattered robes. The being's skeletal hands, although they weren't actually bone, were clutching a nasty-looking scythe. It was Death. She had no doubt of it.

"What is it, my friend?" Father Time asked the new arrival.

Death lifted his scythe and pointed at it Molly. The blade was two feet from her nose. "Is she the one?" he asked. His voice was eerily soft and calm.

Father Time nodded. "Yes. She is the one we have chosen."

"Have you asked the Dream Keeper, or the Gate Keeper?" Death asked in a whisper. "Or are you acting on the Creator's behalf?"

"The Creator had a hand in this," Father Time admitted. "But the final decision was given to me. Is that why you have come? Or is there something else you wish to know?"

Molly was still shocked by the presence of Death and looked on uncertainly, and with a fair amount of trepidation.

"I have been *busy*," Death replied crisply. "Like never before. Death has come to many. It is time she *began* her journey. Before I am the only one who is *needed*," he finished in what Molly thought sounded like a threat.

Death looked at her. She could not see his face, but she knew that he was looking her over very carefully. "I shall see you again," he said to her in a pleasant way that Molly found completely terrifying. And then he vanished.

"Death is very dramatic," Father Time said in an almost apologetic way. "That is his nature."

The entire time she had been in this room, the girl standing behind her had said nothing and had not moved. Molly assumed it was because she was some kind of errand girl.

Molly regained her composure, determined to stay focused. "So, now I know of at least five of the Keepers. You, Death, Mother Nature, the Dream Keeper, and the Gate Keeper. Are there any more?"

"No more. We are five," Father Time stated. "But Death is right – your journey must begin soon. Others will help you on your way in good time, but I feel like you are ready and will discover what you need while on your journey. Are you ready to begin?"

"Yes!" Molly said, anxious to get started.

"Very well," said Father Time, handing her the dull crystal sphere. "Much is at stake. And remember, this is not just a dream – this is real, even if your body is sleeping. Whatever happens to you in your time here, or in other Realms and Worlds, will be reflected on your sleeping body back in Littletown."

Molly nodded. "Gotcha. Don't get hurt." She took the dull gray sphere in her hands. It wasn't as heavy as she'd thought it might be. It still did not feel magical, but she'd been told that it wouldn't activate until Mother Nature actually had it in her possession.

Father Time pulled out a leather sack from within his white robes and handed it to her. It was easily large enough to slip the crystal sphere inside and could be cinched at the top with a matching leather cord that was threaded into the sack.

Molly put the sphere in the sack, cinched it, and slung it over her shoulder. Her hands were shaking and her belly felt like it was jumping around inside her. "I'm ready!" she said resolutely.

A small red mitten touched her hand and Molly looked down. The young girl had stepped up beside her.

"This is where we leave you," the young girl said.

Molly realized that the light in the room was coming from where the girl was, but there was no lightbulb, sun, or torch in the room. She didn't let the thought linger.

"Are you a Keeper? The Dream Keeper?" Molly asked the girl.

The girl with the red mittens laughed. "No, Molly, I'm not a Keeper. However, like Father Time, I believe you will find Mother Nature."

"Do you know *where* I can find her?" Molly asked hopefully.

"I do not," the girl replied honestly. "You begin this journey knowing as much about her whereabouts as Father Time or I. Others are on the way. They will assist you on your journey."

"This is freakin' nuts," Molly said, feeling terrified, excited, curious, hopeful, determined, and as ready as she ever would be. "But if I can stop that accident, I can save my father. And it'll be worth it."

The girl looked up at Molly with her mostly black, but still friendly, eyes. They were full of admiration, and touched with what Molly thought was a bit of envy. "You cannot do a thing that was never supposed to happen. You cannot fix a timeline, but simply set it in the correct place," the girl said with absolute assurance. "As we suspected, you are the one."

Molly was starting to believe that herself. This felt important. She had not been expecting something so massive when she'd started seeing things in her painting, or when Brian had said he'd seen her father beside her at school – as if he was still alive. But it was all falling into place.

The blizzard, the golden pocket watch, and Mother Nature. Knowing that there were billions of Worlds and Realms, and in one of them, something had happened to Mother Nature, put it all in perspective. Something had gone wrong, and it was time to make it right.

The young girl raised a hand and pulled off the mitten on her right hand. The small fingers inside looked white and delicate, as if they had rarely seen the light of the sun.

"I will see you after you have found Mother Nature," the girl said. "Please hurry."

The girl made a flicking motion with her exposed fingers and Molly suddenly felt like she was being thrown backward at a great speed as she was plunged into darkness.

Chapter Six

The wind around Molly died down. She found herself standing on a dirt road that stretched far into the distance in front of her, and behind her. The sky was pink along the horizon and violet directly above her, even though there was no sun in the sky to provide the light. On her right and left were large fields of short grass as far as she could see. That was it. Colorful, but plain.

After taking in her surroundings, Molly realized that she was wearing the canteen and pouch that had been in her dreams – the ones that had appeared on the grass mound when the girl had said that Molly would need to be prepared. The leather sack with the crystal sphere was still slung over her shoulder, tucked under her left arm. She was also wearing the clothes that had appeared. They were comfortable enough, and Molly didn't mind.

The shirt she was wearing had short sleeves and felt silky. It hung loosely and Molly thought it was similar to wearing a blouse, although it did not have buttons. It was white, plain, simple, and she thought it looked good on her. The pants were like jeans and also fit her well. They were grey and just as simple and plain as the shirt. The shoes were closer to boots with heavy duty, yet very lightweight, treads. The laces were tied, which was something she found interesting. This dream place may be real, but she found it odd that she didn't have to physically dress or tie shoelaces. Then she realized that maybe she simply *thought* the clothes on herself... She shook her head. Crazy stuff. She also noted that her glasses were back on. Molly shrugged and made a sound like an amused grunt.

She started walking down the dirt road, expecting to come to a town or pass someone along the way. She'd been told that help was on the way. After a while she began to wonder if that was going to happen since the landscape did not seem to change and there was no sign of anything living, other than the grass and herself, and she had been walking for what felt like fifteen to twenty minutes.

"Why bother with making a path if it goes nowhere?" she asked out loud. "Seems kind of pointless," she added, this time a little louder and looking up at the violet sky.

She put the golden pocket watch chain around her head and let the watch drop. It dangled between her small breasts. She stopped for a moment to pick the watch up with her right hand and pop the lid open. The thin black hands were moving very slowly. She counted more than three seconds for every time the second hand advanced. The picture of her family caught her attention and she felt her heart race. *Dad*, she thought lovingly, *I'm going to save you*. She closed the lid and let the watch fall back between her breasts.

She continued walking, but this time she didn't walk as long before stopping. Her mind was posing questions as fast as they came to her.

Isn't someone supposed to meet me? Is this where Mother Nature lives? Did the girl send me to the wrong place? Am I still in the Realm of Timeless Wisdom? Is this some kind of test? Or...a trick?

"Hey!" she shouted. "If I'm supposed to go on a journey, could I get a little help?"

She looked all around her. Nothing. No reply, no wind, no buildings, no people, no change, and no answers. Realizing that she was on her own, she continued on the way she had been going, hoping to find something that would give her answers, or find someone who could help her out.

She walked for another hour, or so she guessed by the slow-moving hands of the pocket watch. The sky began to grow darker and a moon rose in front of her. It was huge, far larger than the one on Earth – since she assumed she was not on Earth.

Annoyed, scared, and a little tired, she stepped off the path and settled down on the grass. For the first time, Molly felt alone. She had no idea where she was or how to get away. Just a short time ago she'd been ready to get underway and now it looked like she was stuck already. She lay down and propped herself up with her arm so she was facing the path ahead.

"Well, it's not like anyone can sneak up on me here!" she said, mostly to break the unnatural silence. Her voice in the stillness sounded strange and frightened her a little, even though she didn't feel like she was in danger.

She looked at the darkening sky along the horizon and the strange stars that were appearing. Many were very large and bright. She hardly noticed how tired she was and gradually drifted off to sleep.

Abruptly, Molly woke up with a start and her eyes shot open. Something had woken her. She was still on the grass beside the dirt path and the stars still twinkled in the dark sky. She was lying on her side and something was nudging at her elbow. She was afraid to turn around. Whatever had nudged her awake, did so again.

What do I do? she asked herself, knowing how exposed she was. It wasn't as though she could run and hide. She was going to have to turn and face the thing, or hope that it went away. *It could be a giant spider!* she thought in fear. *Or, maybe it's just someone sent to help you...* she tried to reason.

"Do you think she's dead?" a soft voice asked, interrupting her thoughts.

"I don't think so," another voice replied. "Why would she come here to die? We're a little late, but not *that* late!"

The voices were male. And even though they had spoken softly, the speakers made no attempt to hide their voices.

If they'd wanted to hurt me, then they probably would have done something already, Molly reasoned. *Just roll over and see who they are*, she ordered herself. She took a deep breath.

"There!" one of the voices said excitedly. "I saw her move!"

Molly forced herself to roll over quickly and found herself face to face with two of the cutest creatures she'd ever seen. They were small horses, about two feet tall, with light feathery wings at their sides. They looked like the Greek mythical creature Pegasus, but were the size of an average dog.

They flapped their wings and flew back a few feet to give Molly room as she rolled over. They looked at her with curious faces. One of the small flying horses was light brown and the other was white with a black patch above his nose.

The white one said, "What are you doing?"

Molly's fear was gone. Now she was curious, and enamored with how adorable the two little creatures were. "Sleeping," she answered.

"I told you," the white one said to the brown one, tossing his mane in pride at being right.

Molly smiled. "You guys are adorable!" she said.

The two horses looked at each other for a couple of seconds and then back at her. "Is that all?" the white one asked. "We're sent here on some huge secret mission and you think we're adorable?"

Molly grinned. She hadn't meant to hurt their feelings, but they sure seemed annoyed by her assessment. "Hey, I just met you!" she retorted. "I don't know what you guys are! And where *are* we?"

The small flying horses rustled their wings and tilted their heads up in a gesture of self-importance.

"What do we *look* like?" the light brown one asked her with a questioning look. "We're Wequen!" he said, as if it should be obvious. "You're at our usual pick-up spot so we can take you where you need to go!"

Molly sat up. "Excellent! I'm trying to find someone."

"Naturally," the white one said. "Who?"

"Mother Nature," Molly replied. "She's gone missing and I have to find her."

The small white flying horse did not move, but the light brown one shook his mane and neighed in a short burst that Molly took as a laugh or a snort. "You're sure about this?" he asked, with eyes far more intense than any she'd seen on a horse before. "You're not…confused, eh?"

Molly wrinkled her brow and lifted up an extended index finger as she prepared to give the little horse a piece of her mind.

"Oh, leave her alone," the white horse said to his companion. He leaned toward Molly, looking her over carefully with scrutinizing eyes, as he asked, "You must have something important for her, right?"

Molly held up the sack with the crystal sphere. "I need to give this to her. It's a new crystal sphere. Father Time and that little girl told me that she can't use her old crystal sphere anymore and that's why the weather is starting to go crazy. As soon as I get this to her, she can help restore things."

"Sounds reasonable enough," the white horse said. "Only, Mother Nature doesn't stick around one place. She goes from World to Realm to World…constantly. It could be difficult to catch up with her, and may take some time."

The brown horse stepped in front of his partner and narrowed his eyes. "Who *are* you?" he asked in a skeptical voice. "Father Time talks to you. You're wearing one of those magic pocket watches. And you are supposed to be worthy of carrying Mother Nature's *actual* crystal sphere…Who *are* you, exactly?"

Molly rolled her eyes. She didn't want to explain herself, or feel the need to prove herself. "I'm Molly Parker," she replied curtly. She set the crystal sphere down and lifted up the pocket watch. She popped the lid and turned it so that they could see the small photograph of her family. "That's my mom and dad," she said.

The light brown horse lifted a hoof and pointed it at the photo. "I've seen him somewhere before. Looks familiar. You're his daughter, eh? Maybe you're telling the truth."

"You saw him?" Molly asked, getting a little excited. "Where? When?"

"I don't remember," the brown horse replied. "I think we saw him here, though. A little while ago. Last season, maybe before that." He looked at his partner. "Do you remember?"

"Hmm… Yes. That was an interesting meeting. He didn't like it here much. Said he wanted to go back or something. We see a lot of Travelers. I only remember him because he was so…excitable. Must run in the family…"

Molly gave him a fake smile. "Thanks," she said. "Now, you know my name, what's yours?"

The animals looked away from the watch. First at each other, and then up at her. "Names?" they asked in unison.

"Yeah," Molly said. "Names. My name is Molly Parker. And you guys are called…?"

"Wequen!" they replied in unison again, but this time with a burst of enthusiasm.

"You both have the same name?" Molly asked, thinking they didn't understand the question.

"We are *all* called Wequen!" the light brown horse said proudly.

"We're *special*. We can Travel without using the gateways. Tele-portation." He winked at her, which she found was the most adorable thing the creatures had done yet, and then he said, "That's our *special* ability."

"We're kind of new," the white horse said. "But you didn't know that, did you?"

Molly shook her head. "No," she replied. "I didn't know that. I don't know anything about you guys, or where the heck I am. I don't even know what World this is."

"It isn't a World at all," the light brown horse said proudly. "Barely even a Realm. It's just a place for Travelers to wait, before they get picked up by Wequen."

"I think I'm starting to get it," Molly said, her mind putting the pieces together. "You can help me Travel, but you're young and haven't been doing…this…for more than a few months." She thought about the one year anniversary of her father's accident. "Maybe a little more than a year."

"Years are different on different Worlds and Realms," the white horse stated. "So, I'm not sure how long it's been. Seems like you *are* getting it, though."

Molly nodded. "OK. Well, I don't care if you haven't been given names yet. I think it's time you had them. It'll be easier for me."

"No one has offered us names before!" the white horse said. "But there's this delicious grass that grows on the white hills of the Rheene Range," he said wistfully. "If I were to be called anything, I would like to be called, 'Rheene.' Brings up good memories, you know?"

Molly smiled and held out a hand as she let go of the pocket watch. "Then you are Rheene," she said matter-of-factly. "Glad to meet you, Rheene."

He bowed to her slightly and tilted his head so he could rub his nose on the back of her fingers.

Molly laughed.

"Did I do something funny?" he asked, clearly confused by her sudden outburst.

Molly shook her head. "Not really. You're just so...adorable!" She looked at the light brown horse and asked, "What about you?"

"Well, I guess you can call me Rheene, too," he said, looking at his partner, and quite satisfied by his answer.

Molly giggled. "No, no, no!" she said. "I need you to have a *different* name so we don't all get confused!"

"Oh, I see!" the small light brown horse said, nodding.

Molly didn't think he fully understood. "Pick another name, one you like," she said.

"Well..." He looked at Molly, then at his partner, and then back up at Molly. "We took that Delmore fellow to the Gossamer Caves a little while ago...he was wearing one of those magic gold watches come to think of it..." He thought it over a couple more seconds. "Yes," he said with a firm nod. "Gossamer...I like that name. Now, I can hear it all the time. You can call me, 'Gossamer.'"

"Oh, that's a beautiful name. It sounds delicate. Pretty, too," Molly said, genuinely happy with their choices. "You guys are good at this."

She stood up and looked down at them with a satisfied smile. "Rheene and Gossamer." She put her hands on her hips. "So, now that we have *that* figured out, where do we start looking for Mother Nature?"

"As we said," Rheene explained, ruffling his white feathered wings, "she doesn't stay in one place. The trick is to find out where she was *recently*, and then track her from there!"

Gossamer nodded his brown head. "We could guess wrong a thousand times," he said. "We need a good place to start, or we might not ever find her."

"Well, I pretty much know *nothing* about your Realms. You gotta take me *somewhere*, though!" Molly exclaimed.

Rheene and Gossamer exchanged a look of uncertainty.

"You thinking about the Tree?" Gossamer asked his partner.

"No," Rheene admitted. "But it's better than my idea, and a good a place to start!"

Molly was making sure her supplies were slung around her shoulder firmly as the two small flying horses decided.

The two Wequen flew up into the air just above her head. "Touch his hoof with one hand," Rheene told her. "And then, while still touching his, touch my hoof with your other hand."

Molly, curious and nervous, reached up slowly and, not knowing what to expect, took hold of Gossamer's hoof between her left index finger and thumb. Gingerly, she touched Rheene's back hoof with her right index finger. Instantly, she was surrounded by darkness.

Less than a second passed. Suddenly, bright sunlight shone through trees that had appeared around them, spreading its dappled light on the forest floor.

"You can let go now," Rheene said. "We're here."

As Molly looked around at the thick forest around them, the two small horses flew to the ground and then folded up their wings. She noticed that her glasses were back on.

"That was wild!" Molly said. "I barely felt it."

"Our *special* ability," Gossamer said proudly. "Teleportation. We're professionals."

"So, where *are* we?" Molly asked.

"The Realm of Flora," Rheene replied. "Mother Nature comes here often. We may find out where she is, if the Tree has seen her recently."

"Think of it as Mother Nature's personal garden," Gossamer added. "The Creator made this Realm so Mother Nature could hone her skills, I think. We like it here. Lots of great places to eat."

"Indeed!" Rheene agreed.

Molly opened her pocket watch and looked at the second hand. It was moving fast, three or four times faster than normal. "Well," she said. "Lead the way."

The two small horses trotted off through the forest and Molly followed. A minute later the forest opened up into a clearing. At the center of the clearing was a tree. It was huge and gnarled. The trunk was ten feet thick at the base and it reached up as tall as a three story house. The leafy branches canopied out in an immense mushroom shape, shading much of the clearing. They walked up to it and Rheene stepped forward.

"Excuse me," he said in his soft voice. "We need your help. We're trying to find Mother Nature."

The Tree's branches shook. Molly was a little surprised when the Tree answered in a rich, lush, voice, "Mother Nature? Is she in trouble?"

The Tree had no mouth, no ears, and no eyes. Not sure if she was supposed to speak, but anxious for answers, she stepped up beside Rheene and said, "She's in trouble. But I can help if I can get to her soon. Before it's too late."

In the short time that they had been in this Realm, the sky had become cloudy, and now a mist was forming in the clearing.

"I feared that was true." the Tree groaned. "The weather has been strange, and the land's speech has been inconsistent. I have been here from the beginning and only then was it so. Only then did the land cry out in such confusion…"

Molly thought it was the Tree who sounded confused.

"Do you know where she was before this happened?" Gossamer asked hopefully.

"She is a Keeper," the Tree replied. "She will come to you."

"Not if something *bad* has happened to her," Molly said.

"Aren't you supposed to know these things?" Rheene asked the Tree.

Molly suddenly realized just what the Tree really was. "You're the Tree of Knowledge!" she exclaimed.

"You have heard of me," the Tree acknowledged.

"Well, you're in some of the stories in my World," Molly replied, noticing the mist growing thicker around them. "Religious books, too. But I don't know them too well."

"Are the stories you know good stories?" the Tree asked her.

Molly wasn't sure she wanted to answer. The Tree sounded like it might not respond well to hearing anything about stories that might be unpleasant. Fortunately, she didn't have to respond. A bolt of lightning flashed across the sky, startling her, followed by a deafening roll of thunder.

"Yikes!" Molly said, hunching her shoulders.

"It's getting worse!" Gossamer said, shaking his head. "We need to start somewhere else if the Tree doesn't know where Mother Nature is."

Molly was looking at the great Tree and thinking it must have been around for billions of years. How much did it know?

"Never mind about those stories," she said, hoping the Tree would move on. "Do you *know* if Mother Nature is looking for me?"

The Tree of Knowledge shook its branches. "I do not," the Tree replied.

"Do you know if I *will* find her?" Molly asked.

The Tree was still. "I do."

Molly and the two Wequen waited a moment.

"Well?" Molly asked after realizing the Tree wasn't going to say more on that. "Will I?"

The branches shook again. A lightning bolt flickered, followed by a low rumble of thunder. "The answer may change your actions, and therefore must not be spoken," the Tree said firmly.

Molly was not impressed by this ancient being that reportedly housed a massive amount of knowledge. She rolled her eyes and stretched her arms out at her sides. "What *can* you tell me – that will actually help?" she asked in exasperation.

"You are doing what is necessary," the Tree answered in the same firm tone. "What was meant to be will now come to pass – but not in the way any but the Prophetess foresaw."

"What the heck does that mean?" Molly asked. "Am I supposed to see this Prophetess?"

"No," the Tree replied. "Seek the Keeper of Dreams."

"Finally!" Molly and Gossamer said at the same time. They looked at each other. Gossamer winked. Molly grinned.

"I…am growing tired," the Tree said. "Come see me again later, and perhaps I may be able to tell you more…"

Molly wasn't finished though. There was something she'd always wanted to ask someone who was considered wise and she wasn't going to miss her chance. She knew that it was a smart-ass question, but that had never stopped her before.

"What's the meaning of life?" she asked.

This time the Tree of Knowledge laughed. It was a deep grumbling sound, like the thunder, but it was most definitely a laugh.

"The single-most asked question from the dreamers in your World!" the Tree stated. "It is different for everyone, as simple as it is. The meaning of life is to find meaning in it."

Molly was a little surprised. She had been expecting a trite answer, but found that the Tree of Knowledge's answer might have some truth to it. "Huh," she said quietly. "Kinda makes sense."

Rheene flung his wings out and flew up to where he could look at Molly at eye level. "We may get lucky if the Dream Keeper is still around," he said. "I don't want to make your decisions, but we *are* in a hurry, right? We might find the Dream Keeper if we go now."

Molly nodded while Gossamer flew up beside his partner.

"You remember how we do this?" Rheene asked.

"Yep," Molly said, and reached out to touch their hooves.

Chapter Seven

There was a brief moment of darkness and then Molly was hit with a blast of wind. She let go of the horses, stood her ground, leaned into the wind a little, and brought her hands to her eyes to shield them from the bits of dirt, grass, sand, and debris the wind was whipping at her. Her glasses were gone again. She squinted, barely able to see beyond the two small horses flying a few feet in front of her.

"Lovely," she said, barely opening her mouth. A few bits of debris found their way into her mouth and she turned away from the wind to spit them out.

Rheene and Gossamer struggled greatly against the wind. Their wings flapped rapidly.

"We're not far!" Rheene said, turning his small head to talk to her. "Follow us!"

Molly could see just enough of the haunches of the two Wequen leading her to follow, but she could not see her surroundings at all. Suddenly, the wind stopped and the dirt, grass, and other bits in the wind fell to the ground. Molly could see blades of green grass poking up through the inch or two of debris that had settled.

When she looked up, she could see around her for a good distance. A stone house, like a small, plain castle, was only a few yards in front of them. Gossamer had landed at the front door and he knocked on it with a front hoof.

The door opened slowly and a voice from inside asked, "What brings you here, Travelers?"

The door opened fully and a woman stood in the doorway. Molly dropped her gaze from the woman's beautiful face the second she caught sight of it. "Medusa!" she whispered in surprise.

Molly felt a kick on her shin. She looked down to see Rheene looking up at her with disapproval. He lifted a wing to shield his face from Medusa's view. "That's the Dream Keeper!" he said as forcefully and as quietly as he could.

"But I don't want to turn to stone!" Molly whispered back.

Medusa laughed. "Don't be ashamed," she said to Rheene. "On her World I am known to turn men into stone with one look." She lifted her gaze to face Molly. "A misconception, child," Medusa said to her. "As the Dream Keeper, I have been given all sorts of interpretations in various Worlds." She fingered the neckline of her dress that hung a few inches from her thin, but muscular neck. "It helps to keep some of the stories alive. Makes for fewer distractions."

Molly raised her head. Medusa was dressed in a green gown with thin shoulder straps. It was close-fitting, made from delicate fabric, and ended at her ankles. Her skin was light in color, but not pale. She had strong shoulders and stood with her back straight, proud and with authority. There were snakes on the top of her head instead of hair. The snakes were about the size of spaghetti noodles, about a foot long, dangled around her neck, and seemed to sway slightly, almost hypnotically. Their small heads were no larger than the nail of Molly's pinky finger and had Medusa been seen from further away, Molly doubted that she would have even noticed that the Dream Keeper's hair was actually of mass of snakes. Their heads faced in all directions, looking out from around the base of the Dream Keeper's neck. Their minute forked tongues flicked in and out rapidly, as if agitated or taking in as much information as they possibly could. The thin snakes were dark green, darker than Medusa's emerald eyes. Molly thought the Dream Keeper was beautiful. More than that, Medusa was gorgeous and radiant, like a Hollywood bombshell from the 1940's or 1950's. There was a powerful energy radiating from Medusa that she found very similar to what she'd felt from Father Time a short while ago. However, the Dream Keeper appeared to be even more powerful than Father Time.

"What brings you here?" Medusa asked, looking at the pocket watch around Molly's neck with curiosity.

Molly did not like the way the Dream Keeper was looking at the golden watch, and at her. It made her feel a little uncomfortable, as if she was being evaluated. The look was quite similar to the one Father Time had given her when she had met him. It reminded her of what it was like to watch as two peers looked over a group of kids, including herself, as they picked teams for a neighborhood basketball or soccer game. "We're trying to find Mother Nature," Molly replied, transfixed by Medusa's appearance.

Medusa raised a clenched fist. "She's not been doing her duty lately.

I'd like to find her, too." She shook her head and the thin snakes on her head swayed like seaweed in an underwater current. "Come in," she said, standing aside and gesturing with an elegant hand for them to enter. "You can explain yourselves. Perhaps you can help us understand what is happening, as we have been discussing her whereabouts ourselves."

Molly, Rheene, and Gossamer entered the stone structure. It was cozy inside, with a fireplace on the far wall and a few pieces of large, lush, furniture. A brightly-colored hand-woven rug covered most of the stone floor. There was a sofa not far from the door. It had a metal frame that looked bronze and contained white cushions upon which sat two beings. One was a woman far more beautiful than any other woman that Molly had ever seen, and the other was a middle-aged man with a single eye in the center of his forehead. Opposite them, was a being standing in the shadows.

Medusa went and sat between the beautiful woman and middle-aged man with one eye. But Molly could not take her eyes off of the being that stood on the other side of room, facing the three who were seated on the cushioned couch. He was a being of great stature, muscular arms folded over his bare chest. He was only half-man: from the waist down, he was a horse.

It was a Centaur – the same one she'd seen in the painting of Littletown in her bedroom the night before the blizzard hit. He was like a dark god – with a power so clear in his physique and manner that he terrified her in a way that was unnerving. He wore nothing. She didn't think he would hurt her, or that he was even interested in her at the moment. But, the half-man/half-horse being standing with his arms crossed was a massive presence. Molly had seen lions in a zoo once and they were nothing compared to the Centaur standing silently in the room.

Molly knew her mythology. She loved it. She was clearly in the presence of Greek legends – the beautiful woman was a Siren, the one-eyed man was a Cyclops, the Dream Keeper was Medusa, and the Centaur, the most imposing of them all, stood boldly opposite them.

"What will you do when you find Mother Nature?" Medusa asked Molly.

Molly, after a brief glance at the Centaur, took the sack from off her shoulder and pulled out the cloudy crystal sphere. "I need to give her this," she stated.

Rheene and Gossamer watched silently.

"A new crystal sphere?" the Cyclops asked, leaning forward. "What happened to the other?"

Molly shrugged. She wondered if she should be more in awe of her present situation, but somehow it felt normal – as though she was simply showing a new shirt she'd gotten to her friends. "I don't know what happened to her other one," she answered. She looked up at the Centaur, unable to ignore his silent, overpowering presence. He intimidated her. She looked back at the Cyclops and his single eye. "Father Time doesn't seem to know either," she explained. "He just said that he needed someone to Travel the Worlds and Realms to find her, since she's gone missing. The weather is going crazy and things could get really bad, although it seems pretty bad right now back home. Here, too. Anyway, Father Time's going to let me go back in time a year so I can save my dad – if I can find Mother Nature and get this to her." She shrugged again and shook her head. She wondered if she'd said too much, but Rheene and Gossamer had brought her here with the intention of finding out where Mother Nature was. "That's all I know." She put the sphere back in the sack and cinched the opening shut.

"That's about all we know, too," Rheene added from beside her.

"I have not seen Mother Nature for some time," the Centaur said in a rather plain voice, stepping closer to Molly.

Molly turned, taking the opportunity to look the magnificent being over more carefully. He was eight feet tall, at least. It was hard to tell for sure since he looked so imposing. His horse-half was sleek, dark brown, and shone brilliantly as if he were a well-kept racehorse. The Centaur's tail swished a little, back and forth, as if he was thinking about something deeply. His human-half was larger than any man she'd ever seen. His muscles seemed almost impossible, enormous and ripped like a body builder. She had no doubt that a single backhand swipe from him could kill almost anything. However, in contrast to his physical presence, there was kindness and thoughtful reflection in the Centaur's eyes. He looked no older than thirty years at first glance, but Molly could tell he was far older than that. Not just strong, but wise and knowledgeable.

"Could you track her?" Medusa asked the Centaur.

He uncrossed his arms and put his hands on his waist, just above his horse-half. "Perhaps. It isn't tracking skills that are needed here, though," he said, looking directly at Molly. "Would you mind my company?"

Molly swallowed. She was frightened of him, but if he was going to be with them, she thought their chances of taking care of any 'problems' just went up to almost one-hundred percent. "We're just getting started," she said, looking down at Rheene and Gossamer. "What do you guys think?"

The two Wequen were awed by the Centaur, but they did not look to be as intimidated by him as Molly was.

"Absolutely!" Gossamer said. "It would be an honor, Owen."

Rheene nodded quickly in agreement.

"You know this guy?" Molly asked them.

They were about to answer when the Cyclops cut them off.

"If Mother Nature has lost her crystal sphere, then who knows what perils are ahead," he said. His single eye blinked. "If she knew you had that," he pointed to Molly's sack, "she would have found you already – if she was able."

"It explains the tidal waves," the Siren said in a luscious, full voice. There was genuine concern in her beautiful tone. "And the sporadic water spouts. It is a dangerous time, indeed, with a Keeper unable to maintain control."

"But what would cause it?" the Cyclops asked.

"Who," the Centaur corrected.

Medusa looked at him. "I agree, Owen." She turned to look at the golden pocket watch dangling from Molly's neck. Her emerald eyes narrowed. "Since Father Time seems to think this young woman is capable, maybe it is best if you went along." She looked at Molly with her intense eyes.

Molly felt naked as the Dream Keeper locked eyes with her. It was as if Medusa could see through her, into her past, into her dreams, and to the core of who she was.

Molly was surprised when the Dream Keeper suddenly broke out in an honest smile. It was a relief, like Molly had been on trial for murder and just been found not guilty of all charges.

"You are resourceful," Medusa said, narrowing her eyes. "Strong. Even stronger than..." her smile faded a little as she looked up at Owen. The Centaur was stoic, his face expressionless.

The room was silent for a few seconds. Molly wasn't sure if she should say something. Rheene and Gossamer had gotten rather quiet since they had come in. She guessed that was because they knew that these beings were in charge here and she followed their example. They were here for advice, after all.

"What do you see?" Medusa asked, turning to the Cyclops on her right.

Just then, the winds began to pick up again. Fat raindrops smacked against the windows and a distant roll of thunder shook the windowsills.

The Cyclops stood and closed his eye. He breathed evenly a few times. "I cannot see the outcome," he said slowly. "As though I am able see a timeline yet to take hold...events that alter the web...changing its own nature." He opened his eye and looked at Molly. "I do not see success, or failure. Only that many pieces, some hidden, are being moved that will alter every aspect of existence itself. What lies ahead is unclear to me."

Medusa turned back to Molly, her green eyes no longer looking into her, but at her. "The Tree of Knowledge sent you here," she said. "But not because I can help you. It was Owen you came for. You will need him." She pointed at the pocket watch. "You bear the token. You wear it with an easiness that I have not seen before. You feel its *true* potential."

For the first time, Owen shifted his weight, his large hooves making a heavy sound on the rug beneath him.

Molly was not sure she fully understood what the Dream Keeper meant, but it was obvious that it was something Owen considered profound. Molly thought that the golden watch was just something that allowed her to Travel between Worlds and Realms. But now it was becoming clear that Mother Nature's disappearance was even more serious and disconcerting than Father Time had suspected. Molly realized that Medusa, the Dream Keeper herself, was unsettled. Maybe the Dream Keeper was wondering if she would be the next Keeper to go missing.

Medusa lowered her hand and only flicked her eyes at the Centaur briefly before continuing. "Listen to Owen's council. He has insight that will be invaluable. He is my right hand, a being of action in the Worlds and Realms. Trust him, and your instincts. Mother Nature *must* be found. The Keepers must maintain control."

Molly didn't think it was fear in Medusa's words, but something very close to it.

As if all was decided, Owen stepped forward and looked down at Molly. "You will ride," he said. He offered a hand and Molly took it without hesitation, surprising herself. As if she were no heavier than a box of tissues, he picked her up and sat her on his back.

"The nymphs are the most likely to have seen Mother Nature recently," Medusa said, standing. She looked down at Rheene and Gossamer. "They are not far from here. Owen will lead you."

The Centaur walked over to the door as the Dream Keeper opened it wide. Molly looked back over her shoulder at the Cyclops and Siren. They were watching her with concerned looks. She turned back to face the open doorway and saw that the wind had picked up. The rain was not heavy, but the wind was driving it hard.

"Ugh," Molly said. "I don't like wind."

Owen exited the stone building as Rheene and Gossamer flew beside him.

"I will do my best to be patient," Medusa called out after them.

Owen raised his right hand in response, but did not speak. The door closed behind them and the Centaur began to trot.

They had only been outside a few seconds, but Molly realized that the wind was not affecting her. It was as if they were inside a bubble about twenty feet wide that protected them from the wind storm. The two small horses were flying beside her easily.

"That's incredible!" she exclaimed. "How are you doing this?"

The Centaur turned his head and spoke over his shoulder. "It is part of a Centaur's power. As Medusa's chosen soldier, I am immune to many of the annoyances that would hinder me. I am more effective this way, like the other Centaurs, although my power is greater than the rest." He spoke calmly and without pride, explaining his ability as though it were nothing more than hair color.

The winds weren't as strong as when she had first arrived with Rheene and Gossamer. She could see the hills around them and a river that ran by the small stone castle. Owen was following the river as it ran downstream.

"Do you live here?" Molly asked. "In that little castle?"

The Centaur shook his head. "No one resides there. It is a meeting place for Medusa's council for the most part," he explained. "The Cyclops spends more time there than the rest of us. It is a convenient meeting place, with spells guarding it from unwanted visitors."

The more Owen spoke, the less Molly was intimidated by him. He was still impressive, knowledgeable, and a powerful sight to behold, yet he gave her the impression that his kindness was his most prominent attribute. He wasn't rude or arrogant. It was in that moment that she realized she was starting to like him. Not in the same way she *liked* Brian Carter, but in a friendly way.

"How did you get the name, Owen?" she asked him. "It's not too common in my World. I've never known anyone with your name. Do you know what it means?"

She was still surprised by how little Rheene and Gossamer had spoken since they had encountered Medusa and her council. They kept looking at Owen as if he was a rock star.

"Young Warrior," Owen stated, "A Centaur does not age and is a soldier. I was specifically created to enforce the laws of the Worlds and Realms. The Creator has Keepers. Keepers have Centaurs."

They followed the river for a few minutes until they came upon a lake. The winds had died down and the rain stopped. Clouds were still overhead, but now it was growing colder. Rheene and Gossamer went over to the lake and took a quick drink. Rheene stretched his wings and then folded them back up.

"Do we wait for nightfall?" Gossamer asked, looking up at Owen.

The small horse still had a look of awe on his small face as he gazed up at the powerful Centaur. "Nymphs can be touchy if they're interrupted."

Owen nodded. "We will go to the forest edge and wait a short while before entering. No need to startle them."

They made their way around the lake, Owen out in front at a gallop and Rheene and Gossamer flying beside him, keeping up easily. Molly was glad she was riding. Even though she liked running, it seemed as though they were going to be doing a lot of walking and running, and riding made it easier on her. She wondered how long the little horses could keep up.

"How big is this Realm?" Molly asked. She was naturally curious and became talkative when she was nervous, or out of her element.

Owen didn't seem to mind. "The Realm of Timeless Wisdom is the largest of all Realms," he answered, as if he'd been asked the question many times before. "Many of your Worlds could fit inside it, although a Realm is not spherical. Realms were separated from Worlds when Death was created. The division makes it difficult to explain fully. The vastness of any Realm is like the mind of a powerful wizard. The vastness of the Realm of Timeless Wisdom is more like an actualization from the imagination of the Creator. Not as changeable as the Dream Keeper's Realm, but some Realms grow and change as if living things. This Realm is one such place."

"Cool," Molly said, impressed at how easily she understood him. "So, it's like being *inside* the Creator's mind."

Owen laughed slightly, startling Molly a little. "Well said," the Centaur praised her. "That is as good an explanation as mine, only shorter."

They reached the edge of the forest. Molly looked up at the darkening sky. While it had gotten a littler darker since they left the small stone castle, the air had not gotten any colder. She was glad of that. There was a bright silvery moon rising on their left and another one, yellow-orange, cresting beside it.

"You have two moons here?" Molly asked the Centaur.

"On this night," he replied, looking into the woods. "Sometimes there are none, and, when the alignment takes place, there are six. That will be coming soon."

It was dark among the trees. Owen had only paused for a moment. Slowly, he started in. Rheene and Gossamer followed, this time trotting behind him. It grew darker rapidly among the trees. Molly looked around at the trees. They did not seem any different than trees on Earth.

A face! Molly thought suddenly. *I saw a face in that tree!*

Something rustled behind them. She twisted around to see behind her.

"What was that?" she asked sharply.

Rheene and Gossamer had jumped at the rustling sound and now flew beside her, looking wild-eyed as they searched for what had made the sound.

"I think something's following us," Molly said, hardly above a whisper.

"They have been hiding around us since we entered. What can you see?" Owen asked, still moving slowly, as they went deeper into the forest.

Molly squinted as she leaned back and forth to see through the tree trunks. Faces were peering out from behind the trees.

Owen stopped.

"What are you doing back there?" he asked gently, turning around.

Molly turned and leaned over to see around Owen's muscular shoulder. A group of youthful-looking women, about twenty yards away, began to emerge from behind the trees. Not just faces, but frightened faces. The short women had unusually large eyes, made even wider in their terrified state. Most were scantily dressed, a few were naked. They were thin and looked pale, unnaturally so.

"We are frightened!" one of them replied in a shaky, but pleasant voice.

"What has frightened you?" Owen asked, taking a step closer to them. They were only a dozen yards away now and Molly counted forty-four of them.

"We cannot speak to the land as we once did," the same one replied. "There is...a...*distance* between us and the land. Something is *wrong*. The land is *unwell*. We are growing weaker. What is happening?" She was pleading with the Centaur, confused and frightened.

"You have no need to fear us," Owen said comfortingly, walking closer to them. "Mother Nature may be in danger and we are searching for her. Her control has been disrupted and nature has become unbalanced. It must be affecting you more than most."

The small, wispy women came up to them, bunched together and looking up at the Centaur hopefully. She noticed how they looked at Owen with respect and knew that his reputation had preceded him. The nymphs assumed he was here to help, but were so weak and frightened that they had remained hidden until he had asked them to come out.

Now that they were a few feet away and in a semi-circle in front of them, Molly could see them quite well. Some were five feet tall, others just four. Their skin was smooth and dark brown. They all had long, light brown or blond hair that dangled around their waists or ankles. The light fabric dresses that most of them wore fluttered in the breeze. They looked tired and hungry, as though they had not slept or eaten for days.

"We have been hiding," one of the other nymphs said. "Mother Nature has not tended us recently. We listen to the trees. We have tried to hear what the wind is saying…but the trees are silent and the wind sends us confusing messages. We could see you coming, Owen, but we weren't sure if you came to help us. This is a terrible time, full of uncertainty!"

"I will find Mother Nature," Molly said to them. "She might not know it, but I have a new crystal sphere for her and when she gets it, things will go back to the way they should be." She meant it for them – and for herself, as she still fully intended to make good on her promise to Father Time, and get the chance to save her father.

"It is worse than Medusa expects if you cannot communicate with the land," Owen said gravely. "It is almost certain that Mother Nature is in terrible danger."

The nymphs murmured among themselves for a moment and then the littlest of them stepped forward. "We may not be able to help you find Mother Nature, but we do know-"

There was a loud crash that startled everyone. A few of the nymphs screamed. One of them vanished in a flash. Another loud crash shook the forest, even closer.

Molly could feel Owen tense under her. It was barely noticeable. She got the impression that he was just as startled as the rest of them, but did not want to show it.

"Run!" he shouted at the nymphs. He swept his hand in a scattering motion. "Flee from the sounds. Run!"

Molly didn't know what was coming, but whatever it was, it seemed to be massive. The ground began to rumble and the trees shook from a tremendous force. Rheene and Gossamer flew closer to the Centaur, their faces as terrified as the nymphs.

"What is coming?!" Rheene asked Owen, who was slowly backing away from the sounds of crashing trees.

And then, suddenly, it was quiet. Molly could hear some of the nymphs crying as they fled. She was on full alert, eyes wide and heart pounding as she looked around the forest.

"What do we do now?" Rheene asked Owen.

"This is something new to me," the Centaur replied, sounding like he might know what had been out there, but too frightened to say so. "I have not experienced the like before," He paused, looking at a few of the nymphs who were returning to them now that the crashing had stopped. "I think it is time to leave." He stepped toward one of the nymphs and held out a hand with his palm up. "You were saying something before the disturbance. I think it might have been something to help us in our search."

The nymph shook her head. "To the gateway…" she said quietly, looking defeated. "But is far…so far…"

"Not far for us!" Gossamer said. "Rheene and I can teleport all of us out of here if we know where we're going!"

The nymph looked hopeful.

The sound of splintering wood echoed through the forest. It was twice as loud and closer this time. It was as if the trees weren't just being toppled, but exploding. A tree trunk behind them blew apart and the top half crashed down. Owen leaped forward to avoid it, but the nymph was not fast enough. She was crushed, vanishing as the treetop landed on her.

Another tree fell, crashing in front of them. Molly could see black shapes among the trees. They looked round but she couldn't see them clearly enough to tell what they were. The toppled tree fell on two nymphs, who also vanished as they were crushed. Molly screamed. Rheene and Gossamer were darting back and forth around her in a near state of panic. It had only taken a few seconds, but what had started as a trip to find nymphs had turned into a war zone.

"Run!" Owen shouted at the remaining nymphs again, waving his arms wildly. "Run!"

Molly had never been more terrified. Her blood was pumping, heart pounding, as the forest was being torn apart around them. The ground shook as if being ripped apart by a powerful earthquake. It was difficult to see clearly in the dark, even with the two large moons. Trees were splintering and she could see pieces of bark flying through the air.

Owen spun around. Ten yards away a tree lifted up from the ground as if something was pushing it up from underneath. The tree fell toward them. The Centaur threw his arms up and caught the huge tree and threw it to the side, careful to avoid hitting any of the remaining nymphs. Molly was impressed by the Centaur's strength. Lifting her on his back had been one thing. Throwing a tree aside was another.

"Run!" Owen shouted again.

Now they could see what had pushed the tree up. It was a massive black bubble that was still rising up into the night sky. It did not reflect light, but sucked it in, remaining pure black – far darker than anything around it. There were more, moving at different speeds and in different sizes. They moved wildly, unpredictably. They randomly changed speed, size, and trajectory. That was why some trees fell, while others exploded. It was why the ground shook: as the black bubbles grew, shrank, and rose up from under the ground, darting from side to side, they ripped apart the landscape.

Owen was leaning back and looking at the scene in disbelief.

"Chaos," he whispered. "How?"

He was the only one there who knew what was happening. Medusa had told him once, that before the Worlds and Realms came into being, Chaos existed. The Creator had made the Keepers to keep Chaos away, so the Worlds and Realms would be safe from Chaos's destruction. But with Mother Nature's disappearance, and mostly likely in grave danger, Chaos had returned. Owen knew that the black spheres of devastation were impossible to stop without Mother Nature's aid. He watched in horror as one of the spheres grew larger as it rushed toward them at an incredible speed.

Chapter Eight

Owen didn't wait for the giant black bubbles to get any closer. He spun around and darted after the fleeing nymphs and Wequen. Molly wrapped her arms around the Centaur's waist and held on tightly, eyes closed. More of the black bubbles rose up through the land, toppling trees and rending the ground. The Centaur rode fast, Molly's hair streaming behind her, and he quickly distanced them from Chaos and its destruction.

When he slowed, they were over a mile from where they had been and the sounds of breaking trees and earth were distant, if still unsettling.

"They were…like black hole bubbles," Molly said. "Black, empty."

"Chaos," the Centaur said in disbelief. "I have never seen it before, though I know of it. Without Mother Nature's control, it has found a way through – to here. Perhaps a split in reality, a break in the space between Worlds and Realms…Chaos *has* returned…"

"Father Time didn't say anything about Chaos," Molly said. "It seems like things are way worse than anyone thinks."

Owen nodded. "It is." She couldn't see his face because she was sitting behind him, but she could hear the fear in his voice. "But our mission has not changed, only given more urgency."

As if it wasn't urgent to start with, Molly thought. But she kept it to herself. "What do we do now?" she asked the Centaur.

"We find the Wequen," Owen replied. "I just hope those two haven't fled very far."

Molly was listening to the night. It had suddenly grown quiet. "I don't hear anything now...is Chaos gone?"

"If Chaos was predictable, then it would not be Chaos," Owen said curtly, but not meanly. "I hope some of the nymphs survived," he added somberly.

A frightened voice came from the darkness. "I'm still here!" a nymph said, clutching a tree trunk a dozen yards away.

Owen and Molly turned to face the nymph who had spoken. The moons were a little higher and Molly could see a little better now. Her eyes were also adjusting to the night. "How did you get this far?" Owen asked the trembling nymph.

"I was on my way to join them..." the nymph said. She was hunched forward, tears glistening in her eyes, using the tree to help her stay up. "Sasha, Naomi...dead!"

Owen walked over to her. "I am sorry," he said gently.

The nymph wept. "We have been broken! We are dying with the land..."

"What is your name?" Owen asked her calmly.

The nymph looked up at him. She was slender and pretty. Her large brown eyes were wild. She was just over four feet tall and wore a small, thin dress that loosely covered her from neck to thighs. Her bare toes dug into the dirt as she played with her long blond hair. "Lorania," she answered.

"We can put an end to this, Lorania," Owen said to her firmly and gently. "But we need to find our companions. Two Wequen."

Lorania nodded. "I can hear them, closer to the lake," she replied.

"Climb on," the Centaur said to her. "You will come with us."

Lorania nodded again and climbed on Owen's back, in front of Molly. The nymph was like a child, and Molly put a hand around Lorania's waist. "It's going to be alright," Molly whispered to her.

As soon as Lorania was settled comfortably, the Centaur headed back the way they had come. He galloped at a quick pace. They did not hear any more signs of Chaos through the forest on the way, but the evidence of its presence was all around them. Owen maneuvered deftly around fallen trees and fresh mounds of turned earth.

When they arrived at the lake, the moons had risen and the light was strong enough for Molly to see fairly well. It reminded her of how well she could see on clear winter nights under a full moon.

"We thought our tails had been pinned!" Gossamer said nervously as he and Rheene flew over to the galloping Centaur. "We've seen some wild things in our short time as Traveler aids, but we didn't think we'd make it out alive!"

"Rheene and Gossamer!" Molly said happily as Owen slowed down. She was glad to see they were unharmed. "Chaos didn't get you!"

"Chaos?" Rheene asked, tilting his white head a little as he flew beside Molly, a couple of feet away. "Is *that* what that was?"

As frightened as Molly was, she had missed the little flying horses and felt better at having them with her again. "That's what Owen said," she replied.

"I did not know it had form, but from what the Dream Keeper has told me, as she was there at the beginning of our existence, what we just saw was closer to her explanation than any other thing I have come across," Owen said. "Random and unstoppable. Destructive and changeable." He stopped and looked at the hovering horses. "I know that you do not use them, but we need to get to a gateway. There is one close by."

"Yes, not far," Lorania added, sounding stronger. Molly assumed it was because being around the Centaur, even in their dire circumstance, gave the nymph strength. It was almost tangible.

"Where is it?" Rheene asked the nymph.

"Between the mountains in the Valley of Heather," Lorania answered quickly. "East of the lake."

"I know of it," Owen cut in. "You will see it in my thoughts."

"You know what to do," Rheene said to him in a serious tone. The two small horses flew closer to the Centaur and he reached out to touch each of them. Instantly, without the brief moment of blackness Molly had seen before, they found themselves in a field of vibrant heather that stretched for miles. Mountains rose up from the valley before them a few miles away.

"Over there!" the nymph exclaimed, pointing to the left.

A white arch rose up from the heather twenty feet high, not far from where they were. It was carved with symbols that Molly could not decipher, even though she'd been able to understand everyone's speech. She found the large white arch beautiful, the carvings like a cross between Egyptian hieroglyphics and Native American totem poles.

Lorania dismounted and walked up to the arch without talking. She began to sing in a beautiful voice, the melody complex and moody like something from a Russian classical music composer. As she sang, the space inside the archway began to change. It *shimmered*. Molly had been able to see the heather through the arch a couple of seconds ago, but now it rippled like a waterfall had appeared in it, only without any water. The shimmering faded a little and she could see what was through it more clearly: it was like a doorway into another place that had opened when the nymph sang.

A young man stepped through the gateway arch from the place that had appeared when Lorania sang. Molly thought he was about her age, but his questioning blue eyes looked older. He had curly blond hair and full lips. He wore plain, light brown pants and a loose white shirt that was open halfway down his chest. He looked like he'd been woken up by their arrival. Lorania stopped singing. "Yes?" he asked the small group, his gaze lingering on Owen. "Where do you need to go?"

"We are looking for Mother Nature," the nymph said from beside him.

A questioning look passed over the young man's face. "Is that so?" he asked her quietly.

"You are the Gate Keeper," Lorania said hopefully. "Have you seen your sister? Has she used your gateways recently?"

The Gate Keeper looked up from the nymph and then at Molly. Just like with Father Time and the Dream Keeper, it seemed as if he could see right through her. "What are you doing with them?" he asked, flourishing a hand in her direction. He looked like a stage actor to her, his movements and speech exaggerated. "You are not of this Realm."

She leaned over to see him better from behind Owen's large torso. When she did, her pocket watch swung out. It sparkled in the bright moonlight. However, it did not seem a slight thing to the Gate Keeper as he physically recoiled at the sight of it.

"You have one?" he asked. "How? I was not aware!"

Before Molly could try to explain, Owen spoke up.

"Mother Nature is in danger. Father Time chose this one to find her," the Centaur said in a firm voice. "She has a new crystal sphere for your sister. The Wequen brought her to Medusa. But even she is unaware of Mother Nature's current condition. Dire times. Weather is unstable..." he paused before he finished. When he spoke again, his tone was serious, as if giving the worst news possible. "Chaos has returned."

The Gate Keeper recoiled again. "Chaos?" he whispered. His look of sheer terror did not feel like a performance now. Molly had seen what Chaos had done.

"My sisters," Lorania said with a broken voice. "Dead...their memories returned to the wood...lost...Sasha..."

The Gate Keeper put a hand on her shoulder and squeezed it tenderly. "I hear next to nothing in my Hall," he said, frightened and angry. "But if you are seeking Mother Nature, then perhaps it is best you came to me. I have seen her, and not too long ago. If only I had known sooner..."

Owen walked up to the Gate Keeper. Molly could have touched the Gate Keeper if she reached out. The Centaur shook his head and swished his tail.

"No one was warned," he said. "We are caught behind a veil that was thrown over all of our eyes. Yet we stand here now, ready. Where did you see her last?"

"I will take you," the Gate Keeper said without hesitation. "If Chaos has returned, we are out of time already. No more questions."

He turned to face the white arch and began to sing. This was a song unlike the one Lorania had sung. This was a slow song, deep and primal. As he sang, Molly saw the gateway shimmer again, as if through that waterless waterfall, and a new place began to emerge inside the white arch. Beyond was a desert with a bright sun above. The Gate Keeper waved them through.

Lorania got up on Owen's back, settling in front of Molly. The Centaur walked through the gate, Rheene and Gossamer close behind.

"Why do you sing?" Molly asked the Gate Keeper as they passed him.

He looked at her curiously, his eyes darting to her pocket watch a few times. "That is how Travel is done through the gates," he replied. "Music, the universal language. All beings understand, no, *feel*, music, even if they cannot understand the lyrics. Billions of gateways, billions of songs: one unique song for every gate. Some Realms, such as this one, have more than one gate, more than one song."

Even though Molly could tell that he was concerned for Mother Nature and terrified that Chaos was out there, she could tell that he relished talking about the gates and Traveling. "I guess math *isn't* the universal language!" she said. "Or love."

"How often does mathematical and scientific knowledge change?" he asked her with a smile. "How often do 'facts' get altered, or are found to be false after more discoveries?" The Gate Keeper looked to be on stage again, this time as a philosopher.

Molly shrugged. "I don't know," she replied, not realizing that he wasn't looking for an answer. She could feel Owen getting impatient, but he remained quiet for the moment. His tail kept brushing across her back as he swished it.

The Gate Keeper continued on, as if in a performance.

"New discoveries bring change constantly!" He paused for dramatic emphasis. "But the way you *felt* when you heard a song you loved...did that change so much? Or how much love you feel for your mother...or *father*?"

Molly wasn't sure what he meant by the way he altered his voice when he said, 'father.' "I don't know," she said uncertainly. "Those things can change, I guess."

She noticed that her glasses had materialized as they had entered the desert through the arch.

"Music transcends words, even though it is mathematical in nature. It has a far deeper connection to the *essence* of your life than any equation!" the Gate Keeper said, relishing his own words. It was clear that he could go on for a long time. However, Molly also felt that the Gate Keeper didn't get many visitors. He seemed desperate to elaborate, even with the imminent danger of Chaos lurking in the shadows. She felt a little sorry for him.

It was as if he could read her thoughts. He dropped his theatrical manner and said, "Love *is* a universal language." He winked at her and then put on a business-like demeanor. "I shall not detain you longer."

"*Thank* you," Gossamer said sarcastically.

Rheene made a chuckling sound and Owen swished his tail. The Gate Keeper went on seriously, ignoring Gossamer. "Mother Nature was here a few days ago." He tilted his head in thought. "Maybe a week. I don't really remember the exact day. But she *was* here."

"I have an idea about where she was headed," Owen said. "We will return if she is not there."

The Gate Keeper nodded. "If she comes back to me before you do, I will tell her that–" The Gate Keeper stopped abruptly as his attention was suddenly drawn to the sky over the desert. Dark clouds appeared out of the blue and were swirling overhead. A funnel cloud formed and began to descend to the hard-packed dirt of the desert.

"Tornado!" Molly shouted in alarm.

Lightning flashed across the sky and strong winds began to pick up as the twister made its way down from the thick clouds.

Owen took charge. "Can you keep up if I run?" he asked Rheene and Gossamer.

The small horses nodded. Gossamer was keeping a close eye on the tornado as it drew closer to the ground. Molly and Lorania watched it carefully as well.

"I am glad we are not headed in that direction," the Centaur said to himself, although Molly and Lorania overheard him.

Without word or warning, Owen bolted away from the gateway and the Gate Keeper at a tremendous speed. Surprised at the suddenness of speed, Molly grabbed onto Lorania to keep from falling, and the nymph tightly wrapped her slender arms around the Centaur's waist. Molly wondered if Owen was used to having passengers. In a few seconds, they were moving as fast as a car on a highway. Molly glanced over her shoulder to see the Gate Keeper walk through the gate and disappear from sight.

The tornado touched down, kicking up a cloud of dust.

Owen ran from the storm. A short while later, putting a little distance between them and the storm, they arrived at the edge of the desert. The storm was still behind them, heading in their direction. There were two tornadoes now and they were moving faster, and more wildly. They darted from spot to spot, often moving hundreds of yards in a second.

"I thought you were protected from the weather!" Molly shouted at Owen over the sounds of the wind.

"Wind and rain," Owen shouted back. "Not tornadoes!"

Up ahead, mountains stood in the distance. There was a short stretch of green grass and small trees, and then foothills. Molly knew that tornadoes mostly formed over flat expanses of land. She hoped that if they could get to the foothills, or even the mountains themselves, they would be safer. She looked at Rheene, who seemed a little more level-headed, if slightly less humorous, than his partner, and pointed at the mountains. "Can you teleport us there?" she yelled to him.

He was flying behind Owen only a few feet, but she could tell both he and Gossamer were giving everything they had just to keep up. Rheene said something to his partner that Molly couldn't hear and the small flying horses nodded to each other. They put their heads down and flew a little faster to get ahead of the Centaur. Owen reached up and touched each one as soon as they were in position.

Instantly, they were at the base of the mountains, beyond the foothills. Owen slowed down until he was trotting. The strong winds were gone. They were miles away from the storm. Rheene and Gossamer dropped to the ground, exhausted.

"You did it!" She shouted gleefully at them. She looked over her shoulder, but could not see a tornado. The sky was dark, but they were not in any immediate danger.

"Thank you for your quick thinking, Molly," Owen said gratefully. He walked over to Rheene and Gossamer. "I am impressed. You performed well."

Gossamer lifted his head from where he had collapsed and said, "Professionals," between gasps for air.

In spite of the danger, the close escape, the weather getting worse, Chaos returning, and still no clear indication of where the heck Mother Nature was, Molly laughed at Gossamer's comment. She laughed hard.

"Oh, Gossamer!" she said as her laughter faded. "You crack me up."

Rheene, lying beside his partner, swung a wing in Gossamer's direction. "It's his *face*," he said. "Lacks *intelligence*."

The nymph jumped off Owen's back and knelt down beside the little horses. "They need rest," she said.

The Centaur agreed. "It is not safe to be out in the open, though. Carry them," he said, waving a hand at the two fatigued horses. "If I remember correctly, there is a cave nearby where we can rest for a bit."

Molly dismounted, bent down beside Lorania, and scooped up Rheene gently. The nymph picked up Gossamer and they followed Owen as he led them a short way up the mountain. There was a cave with a large opening, but not very deep, and they went inside. Molly and Lorania lay the Wequen down and sat down with their backs against the cave wall.

Molly held up her pocket watch and flipped the lid open. The second-hand seemed to be moving normally. She looked at the photo of her family.

"What is that?" Lorania asked, looking over Molly's shoulder.

"It's a watch," Molly said, moving it closer to the nymph.

"What is it for?" Lorania asked, looking at it curiously with her oversized brown eyes.

"It tells time," explained Molly. "See? It's 4:32."

Lorania looked at both the watch face and the photo. "Why do you need to *tell time*?"

"So we know what time it is," Molly said, looking at her father in the photo.

Owen was standing at the cave opening, looking out. He turned his head toward them and said, "Time is not consistent. Its passage differs from place to place. In one place you may be counting seconds, while another passes years."

"I heard about *time machines* once," Lorania said timidly, sounding like she had never given them much thought. "The nymphs have no such machines. We pass time through seasons, and moons. We grow with the forest, die with the forest, and are reborn in the forest. Why would you need to have a machine that tells you that?"

Molly shrugged. "I guess it's because it helps us get to things when they start," she said. "So we don't miss out on things that only take place at a certain time."

"Like the Dance of the Six Moons!" Lorania said happily, as if she suddenly understood. "It is coming soon! I wouldn't want to miss that!"

Molly nodded absent-mindedly. She was lost in a memory, recalling the day the photo in her pocket watch had supposedly been taken, a couple of months before the car accident that killed her father. She remembered the day, but still could not recall getting the picture taken.

"It's my father I'm looking at mostly," she said. "I guess it's neat to see how time moves differently, but mostly I miss him, and pictures like this, and memories, are all I got."

"I remember Sasha and Naomi," the nymph said sadly. "We entered the forest with our sprouts together. We grew into saplings together... and now they will be reborn with new sisters." She sighed heavily. "If they ever get reborn."

"We will find Mother Nature," Molly said adamantly, snapping the watch closed and letting go of it. "I'm doing this so I can save my dad. I will save him – and fix the timeline."

The Centaur laughed and it startled her. It was a booming laugh, like something she would expect from the Ghost of Christmas Present.

"Timelines are never *broken*," he said. "You took this quest because you wanted your life to be different – even if it takes an...*unusual* route."

"I guess," Molly said, not sure if Owen was joking or trying to be insightful. It didn't feel like he was being mean, although there was a sort of harshness to his words. "But I don't think what happened, the accident, was ever supposed to happen. Sure, I miss him and want him back. I guess I'm doing this for me. But who wouldn't want to go back and save someone they loved? Someone they lost unfairly..."

Lorania grabbed Molly's arm. She looked into Molly's eyes deeply. "I would do almost *anything* for my sisters and the forest," she said passionately. "I don't know much about time machines, fighting, or Traveling, but I know I miss those I love – and who, or what, we love is what matters most in life."

Owen had walked over to them, but Molly had not noticed him as she had been focused on the nymph and her passionate words. He spoke gently and kindly.

"Wise words," the Centaur said. "Now get a little rest. We will need to be on the move soon."

Molly looked over at Rheene and Gossamer as they slept. She didn't think she'd be able to sleep at all. She was too amped up. Still, she took a deep breath, closed her eyes, and leaned back.

Molly felt certain that she had only closed her eyes for a moment, but when she opened them, things had changed. Rheene and Gossamer were awake and over by the cave opening looking up at Owen. They were talking softly. There was a light rain falling outside. Lorania was asleep beside her.

I guess I was more tired than I thought!

Her stomach rumbled loudly. Remembering that she had been given food and drink at the start of the journey, she pulled the three straps free from her left shoulder. Molly set the canteen and sack with the crystal sphere down beside her. She opened the other sack to see what kind of food was inside.

There were a few six-inch-long rectangular boxes inside, two inches high and two inches wide. She pulled one out. It looked like a stack of square crackers. She removed one of the squares and looked it over. It was more like a pastry, a little squishy, kind of like a Fig Newton. It was sealed at the edges so she couldn't tell if anything was inside. She sniffed it (smelled kind of like a berry pastry) and took a small bite from a corner. Liquid shot out onto her tongue, heavy and sweet. It was delicious. She popped the rest in her mouth, and washed it down with a sip from the sweet liquid in the canteen. It was filling. More filling than she anticipated. One was enough for now.

"Better?" she heard the Centaur ask.

Molly looked up. Owen was facing her from the cave entrance. "Yeah." She replied. "But how the hell did I sleep here when I'm asleep in bed back on Earth? That's nuts."

"Your essence is here – what is sometimes called a soul," answered Owen. "You are infinite. Your energy is projecting you here, and that energy, bound to any form, still needs rest. Until your energy is completely detached from your body, it will require all the needs your body does to keep it alive."

Molly thought she understood that. When she died, her sleeping and eating days were over. She glanced at Lorania. The nymph was waking beside her. However, Molly thought Lorania didn't look better after the rest – but even worse.

"Is something wrong?" Molly asked her.

"More of my sisters are gone…" she said weakly. "The forest suffers…" The nymph took a deep breath and blinked her large brown eyes. She shook her long blond hair and gently put a hand on Molly's arm. "But if it's time to go, then I'm ready," she said, resolute. "We *must* find Mother Nature!"

"I'm still concerned about this whole Chaos thing," Rheene said, walking over to Molly and glancing up at Owen. "I know Gossamer and I are new to the Worlds and Realms, but why haven't we ever heard about Chaos before?"

Gossamer was trailing his partner and he nodded in agreement. "Seems important to me. Everyone should be aware of it!"

Molly looked up at the Centaur. "Father Time didn't warn me about it," she said. "I'd like to know a little more before we get to where you were taking us, even though I know we're in a hurry."

The Centaur nodded. "Before I was brought into being, the Creator began to form existence and Chaos was there, a sort of god I suppose, a threat that could undo the Creator's work," Owen said, sounding as though he was still piecing it together. "I was told by the Dream Keeper that there was a battle and Chaos lost. At that point, the Keepers were created to help maintain order. Their existence and power help hold reality in place, as far as I know. Chaos had not been seen since. And due to the Creator being the only being to have come in contact with Chaos, it was more of a legend than actual history. It was only through Medusa that the Centaurs came into being a short while later. However, I have come across many tales in my Travels. More than once the legend of Chaos has been told, and while the tales differ in nature, most point to one thing – if the Keepers lose control, Chaos would return." He paused for a moment. "I feel certain that Chaos is back, and Mother Nature's disappearance is why. I needed time to think these things over, consider our options and chance of success. A small group like ours can travel quickly, and with the Wequen, we can teleport when needed. We are well-equipped for this task. Now that you are rested, it is time to continue our search. We must move as fast as we can. However, we will rest when needed."

Molly opened the sack with the crystal sphere and slipped it out of the bag. "I hope this is worth it," she said, looking at the cloudy sphere. "I hope Mother Nature is alive and that with this she can get rid of Chaos."

"You'd think that the Creator would just get rid of Chaos right now!" Rheene said, sounding very annoyed.

"That's the problem," Owen said. "After the battle, before the Worlds and Realms came to be, much of the Creator's power was given away: some was given to the Keepers, some to the Kreags, some to chosen beings like the Centaurs, and some to every other living thing in existence." He paused. When the Centaur spoke again he sounded troubled. "I doubt the Creator is powerful enough to just push Chaos away again."

"That's comforting," Gossamer said sarcastically. "Not like there's any *pressure* on us!" He shook his mane. "Come on, ladies," he said to Molly and Lorania, "let's get going!"

Molly gathered up her stuff and then she and Lorania got back on the Centaur's back. Rheene and Gossamer walked on either side of Owen as they left the cave. The invisible bubble around the Centaur kept them dry as they crossed the mountain pass.

Owen was sure-footed and moved between a walk and trot. Rheene and Gossamer flew, easily this time as the Centaur moved slower through the rocky terrain.

When they arrived on the other side of the pass, Molly saw something she hadn't expected: a city spread out at the base of the mountains. It looked to be made of stone with towering buildings and bridges. It looked like something out of medieval times. There was a large castle in the center with spires and banners higher than any other structure. A large stone wall encompassed the entire city, which was in an elongated oval shape. She could see movement in the streets below.

As they approached the city gates she could see two guards standing on either side of the gate. The guard on the left side was tall and slender, over a dozen feet tall. She had seen plenty of Giants in movies and in books, but this one was very different. This Giant, who appeared to be male, looked lithe and athletic. He watched them approach with eyes that Molly found startlingly intelligent.

The guard on the right side, opposite the Giant, was an unassumingly small dragon. Green scales covered most of its body and its yellow eyes were as watchful as the Giant's – though not quite as inquisitive.

The two guards did not move as Owen walked up to them. It was clear to Molly that the Centaur's reputation preceded him here, too.

"We are looking for Mother Nature," Owen said to them.

Molly took a moment to look both the dragon, who was not much larger than herself, and the Giant over carefully. They were fantastical beings, but seeing them close up, they didn't just feel real, they seemed normal. It was as if this was how it was *everywhere* but on Earth. Talking trees, flying horses that were two feet tall and could teleport, nymphs, Centaurs, a Siren and Cyclops, dragons and Giants…Earth seemed rather dull now that she'd been here for a bit. Strangely, she felt at home, as if she'd always have Rheene and Gossamer to banter with and Lorania was like her new sister.

Even so, the situation was dire and she listened as the Giant spoke to Owen.

The Giant bent down a little to get a better look at Molly. "I have not seen her for some time," he replied. "Why do you seek her?"

"Chaos has returned," Owen said, not going into an explanation. "Perhaps you have seen the effects?"

The Giant looked wary and skeptical. However, the dragon looked as if he didn't understand.

The Centaur continued, unconcerned by their reactions. "It tore through the nymph's forest in the Realm of Timeless Wisdom not long ago. When we arrived here through the gate, the weather was as unpredictable as it is in other Worlds and Realms. It is imperative that we find her soon. I don't have time to explain further. If she is not here, then we will move on."

The Giant was about to say something when Molly saw his expression change suddenly. His eyes glanced up at the sky and fear was in them. It was just a trace, but it was there – and it looked like something the Giant wasn't accustomed to feeling.

Everyone followed his gaze. But it wasn't the sky that he was looking at, but a black shape that was emerging from the mountains behind them. The ground began to shake and Lorania screamed in terror, turning away from it and clutching at Owen.

The black shape rose and others began to join it.

Chaos.

To Molly, the black shapes looked like rising bubbles in a glass filled with a carbonated beverage. At least at first. The black bubbles of Chaos *almost* had an order to them when they first appeared.

The sounds of crumbling rocks filled the air.

Then, as if to prove that it was truly Chaos, the bubbles began to shoot in different directions as they ripped apart everything they touched.

Chapter Nine

Panic set in. The dragon bolted. The Giant gave Owen one terrified glance and then ran for the stone city. The Centaur, caught off-guard and unable to hear Rheene and Gossamer shouting for him to touch them so they could teleport away, followed the Giant. In two seconds, he passed the Giant and was inside the city walls.

Molly watched as the city's inhabitants scattered on the streets, some dashing into buildings. It was a scene of confusion and fear. There were other Giants in the city, along with a couple of dragons, some people with feathery wings on their backs, little fuzzy beings that looked like bears, and more that she couldn't make out in the scattered confusion. It seemed like the dark-skinned people with wings were the majority of beings here as they outnumbered the others four-to-one.

She only had a few seconds to take it in before Chaos struck. There was a loud crunching sound and bits of stone flew through the air around the fleeing Centaur. Molly let out a yelp as a sharp pain shot through her left arm, just above her elbow. She reached out and grabbed it reflexively. When she pulled her hand away, she saw blood on her fingers. For an instant she wondered if she was bleeding in bed back home. But the realness of the situation, the crashing of stone, the cries of terror, and screams of pain around her pulled her back to the here and now.

A Chaos bubble briefly appeared in front of them, partially inside a four-story building made of massive stone blocks. The second and third-story corner walls were swallowed up by the black sphere, like a huge bite out of a cake, and the interior of the building, now exposed, began to collapse as the Chaos bubble vanished.

Owen ran by it, deeper into the city, toward the enormous castle at the center. The confusion in the city was turning into a scene of pure panic in the chaos and had become a madhouse. Some smaller beings were being trampled by larger ones. Bubbles of Chaos, some the size of a golf ball, others the size of a large house, came and went. Some lingered, some darted, some moved like wild tornadoes, and others hovered as they vibrated.

Molly watched as a being with wings, shaggy brown fur, and long legs dashed passed them and then took flight. Gossamer flew up beside her with wild eyes. He had a couple of small cuts on his rump. She looked around, but did not see Rheene. Lorania, still clutching Owen's waist for dear life, had been protected from the bits of flying debris.

Owen sprinted down the stone street, nimbly avoiding other fleeing beings. Molly could tell that the Centaur was getting his fear under control. His movements were more precise and he was doing better at not knocking into the other beings around them.

Suddenly, right in front of them, another black bubble of Chaos appeared, ripping up through the stone street and throwing more bits of razor-sharp stone fragments in all directions. The shock toppled another building. Molly watched, helpless, as large stones from the toppled structure crushed the beings beneath it as they attempted to escape.

Molly screamed in horror.

Owen stopped quickly, slamming her up against Lorania, just inches away from the black sphere. It was completely black and the surface returned no reflection. She felt empty and hopeless in its presence. Being so close to it, she felt as though it wasn't just destroying the stones, land, and living things, it was also tearing apart the fabric of reality. The Centaur backed up a few feet and then darted around the Chaos bubble, heading off to the left.

Molly saw that Rheene, who had some cuts as well, had caught up with Gossamer. They were trying to get Owen's attention, but in the confusion and the deafening sounds of crashing stone, earthquakes, and screams, they were not successful.

With the Centaur doing his best to avoid debris, Chaos, and collisions, and Lorania clutching him, Molly realized that it was up to her to reach out and touch the frantic Wequen – and get them far away from there. She kept her left arm firmly around the nymph seated in front of her as she lifted her right hand to wave the two small flying horses over to her. They saw her and flew closer to her, doing their best to keep up with the darting Centaur.

Molly knew that she had one chance. She would have to let go of the nymph to touch their little hooves. If she fell… She pursed her lips and concentrated, determined to stay seated and get them out of danger.

Another loud crash came from their left and Molly almost lost her seat. Her heart skipped a beat. She could feel the blood from the cut above her left elbow as it trickled down her arm. Ignoring it, she regained her seat. While she did, she saw a hand sticking out from beneath a large stone. Her heart sank. The amount of destruction here was even more terrible than what she'd seen in the forest. She swallowed hard, refusing to give in to despair.

"Closer!" she shouted to Rheene and Gossamer.

They flew toward her, eyes frantic. A large chunk of stone fell ten yards ahead of them, breaking apart when it hit the street. Molly reached up in an attempt to touch the horses' hooves. She began to lose her seat, slipping backward. She reached out with everything she could muster, fingers spread.

All I have to do is touch them! she thought desperately. *That's all! Just touch them!*

She was slipping more, and Owen was about to jump over a piece of the fallen boulder. Molly focused on the hooves above her head – only a few inches from her outstretched fingers. Owen jumped. Molly lost her balance. In one last attempt, Molly threw herself forward as she fell.

She hit the ground hard. She tried to breathe, but her lungs weren't working right. Molly was looking up at the sky, struggling to take in air. The sky was light blue. Fluffy white clouds rolled by slowly. A sharp pain shot down her back.

I'm dying! Molly thought in confusion. *Is this how it is?* Again, she tried to breathe, disregarding the pain. *I have to reach Mother Nature! I have to make sure things get set right!*

A spasm of pain went through her entire body as she took in a quick breath.

Gossamer was hovering over her, his wings beating rapidly, his little body silhouetted against the light blue sky.

Another spasm shook her as she was able to take a second quick breath.

The nymph was bending over her now. Behind her, Owen came into view, looking down at her with a face full of concern.

Molly took another breath. It wasn't as painful this time, and she slowly began to breathe more regularly. She propped herself up with her arms. Her chest was tight and her head was spinning.

Rheene was at her side, a front hoof lifted to gently touch her forearm. "Are you alright, Molly?" he asked with concern.

Molly looked at him, and then at the landscape around them. They were not in the city, but in a field of tall grass.

Lorania, who was kneeling beside Rheene, broke out into a wide smile of joy. "You saved us!" she shouted happily. "One of those Chaos bubbles popped out right in front of us! If you hadn't been able to teleport us out, we'd have been killed!"

Molly shook her head. It throbbed with pain. She reached up and touched her temple. She'd had the wind knocked out of her before, and knew that that's what had happened. Only, in the dire situation, it was more intense than when it had happened before; when she'd hit a hurdle in track and fallen hard on her back. "I was only trying to get us out of there. Why couldn't Rheene and Gossamer have just touched us first?"

"Teleporting doesn't work unless the Traveler touches *us*," Rheene explained quickly. "Intention is part of the process." He shook his mane and glanced up at Owen. "We were *trying* to tell you that! But *someone* wasn't paying attention."

The Centaur looked a little embarrassed. Molly was more surprised at that look than the boisterous laugh he'd let out in the cave. She doubted that in the billions of years he'd been around he'd been embarrassed many times before – if ever.

"I admit that I am shaken by Chaos's return," he said. "More so than I have let on." His tail swished violently. His look returned to one of concern and he spoke to Molly in a grateful tone. "Thank you. Lorania is correct in saying that you saved our lives."

Molly nodded a little. "You're welcome," she said. Her head was clearing and getting less painful as she continued to breathe easier and deeper. It still throbbed a little, but she knew that she was more scared than hurt. She was also glad her glasses hadn't appeared in this place when they'd teleported, as they might have gotten broken. Her eyesight hadn't changed the whole time, whether she was wearing them or not. The thought of broken glasses made her think of the crystal sphere she was carrying.

Molly reached back and pulled the leather sack with the crystal sphere onto her lap. She pulled out the grayish ball and ran her hands over its smooth surface. No chips or cracks. It surprised her how light the thing was, and that all the jostling hadn't done it any damage. Then again, she guessed that it was probably made by magic.

"Where are we?" she asked Owen.

"I am not certain, but it looks and feels like the Realm of Nattarra," the Centaur replied. "Lots of cats and cat-people in Nattarra, but I do not see any now."

"At least we're away from Chaos," Rheene added with a visible shiver. "I hope we don't run into it again! Nasty stuff!"

Owen grimaced. "Unpredictable. It does what it does."

It sounded as though the Centaur was rather annoyed by things that were not predictable.

Molly put the sphere back in the leather sack and cinched the opening shut. She slung it over her left shoulder, along with the canteen and the sack of those juicy pastries. "I'm not so sure," she said, slowly getting to her feet. Lorania put a delicate hand on Molly's back for support. "I think Chaos isn't as unpredictable as you think," Molly continued. "It seems to be coming after us. Maybe it senses that I have a new crystal sphere. Or, *something else* is drawing it to us…"

Owen tilted his head and swished his tail. "Perhaps. Our goal to reach Mother Nature hasn't changed. And we are all still alive."

"Barely," Gossamer muttered.

"I think Chaos knows about me, about what we're doing," Molly said, smiling at Gossamer's sarcasm. They'd almost been killed just a moment ago and she was glad that she had companions who hadn't given in to the fear that she knew they were all fighting. "Maybe it found a way trap her – or maybe it's already got her."

Lorania shook her head slowly, her long hair brushing from side to side. "I would feel it if she was…gone," the nymph said with distant eyes. "She may be weakened, but she's still out there somewhere."

"Owen is right, though," Molly said as she tried to get a look at the cut on the back of her left arm. "We're all still here and we still have to find her." The cut didn't look too bad. She was glad of that. It stung, but that was tolerable.

Molly looked at each of her companions in turn. Owen's face was uncertain and determined. Lorania looked even weaker than she had in the cave, but she also looked determined, if a little desperate. Rheene and Gossamer stood side by side, their heads held high. Neither one had said anything about their small wounds. They looked adorable still, but they were tough little guys. And as frightened as they had been, they did not seem to be in any hurry to leave her side – despite the disasters they had witnessed.

"Every one of you is in danger if you stay with me on this journey," she said seriously. "I'd understand if you didn't want to keep going with me."

Gossamer neighed loudly. "Leave you?!" he barked, sounding hurt by her suggestion. "We're professionals, remember? And...I kind of like you," he added in a softer tone. "You got spunk."

Rheene ruffled his wings and nodded. "True, I'm scared of Chaos, but we got a job to do, and getting that sphere to Mother Nature could save every World and Realm from it!" He paused to look at Gossamer. "We also have a reputation to uphold."

Molly grinned. Tears welled up in her eyes at their devotion.

"There are no coincidences for us," Owen said simply. "We are together because we are supposed to be together. I will see your mission through, or die in the attempt. My luck has been rather good for quite a long time and I do not think it will run out now."

Molly swallowed the lump in her throat that was a precursor to a good cry. She was deeply touched by their loyalty. She was not surprised when Lorania added her reason for staying by Molly's side.

The nymph had her long fingers pulled into fists and her narrowed eyes looked at Molly as if she was shocked by the idea that any of them had considered leaving her. "You have shown us courage. Father Time gave you that time machine for a reason! I lost my sisters and I would do whatever it took to get them back. I don't know if that can happen now, but unless Mother Nature regains control, I will lose *everything*! You're my new tree. I go with you."

Molly swallowed that lump in her throat again and quickly wiped away the tears in her eyes before they could fall down her cheeks. "OK," she croaked. She took a deep breath. "Let's get going." She looked at Rheene and Gossamer. "Where to now? I don't know where to start."

The two Wequen looked up at Owen hopefully.

Molly thought that they looked like dogs begging for treats.

"Back to the gate," the Centaur said. "Maybe the Gate Keeper has news." Owen swished his tail. "Perhaps he has received word of Mother Nature's whereabouts."

Molly shrugged. "Works for me," she said.

Owen lowered a little so it would be easier for Molly and Lorania to get on his back. "Ladies," he said, as if addressing queens.

Rheene and Gossamer flew up by the Centaur's head. When Molly and the nymph were settled, Owen reached up and touched their small hooves.

Once again, they were at the gateway in the desert where they had last left the Gate Keeper. The sky was clear. Great trenches had been dug by the tornados, and they stretched for miles in all directions. Despite the damage, the twenty-foot tall white arch was still standing.

Lorania began to sing. The space in the gateway shimmered like it had before. The Gate Keeper stepped out and looked at the small group. The gateway closed behind him. "Where is Mother Nature?" he asked as the nymph ceased singing.

"Not here," Owen replied. "And we are no closer to knowing *where* she is. Chaos struck as soon as we reached the city walls. We were fortunate to survive."

The Gate Keeper looked worried. "So where will you go next?"

"I was hoping you heard something while we were gone," Owen said.

"I think she's been captured," Molly stated, looking directly at the Gate Keeper. "We just need a place to start – where she's been recently. If Chaos shows up again, we might not make it."

"She didn't say much when I saw her," the Gate Keeper said. "Mother Nature talks with me from time to time, but she usually just passes through. She was in a hurry that last time, but offered no reason why."

"Maybe Mother Nature was on to something," Molly said, thinking out loud. "If she found out that something wasn't right and went off to investigate, she wouldn't have known what to say even if she'd been asked."

"Perhaps," the Gate Keeper said. "Come into my Hall where I know you will be safe." He began to sing. The space in the gateway shimmered and he ushered them through with a theatrical wave of his hand.

Once through the arch, Molly found that they were in a brightly lit large room, almost like a throne room. There were a couple of dozen large golden chairs with soft red cushions in the Gate Keeper's Hall. There was a high ceiling, and a large plush rug covered the floor.

"So, no one knows anything," Molly said with a harsh edge to her voice, still focused on the task at hand. She was frustrated. The adventure had been disappointing so far, with the exception of her companions, and far more perilous than she ever could have expected. "I'm about ready to go see if the Tree of Knowledge is any help," she finished, her voice dripping with sarcasm.

"At least we'd be doing *something*," Gossamer said.

"Are you serious?" Molly asked the small light brown winged horse. "I was joking."

Gossamer lifted his wings up a little in what looked like a shrug. "So far, the Tree seems to know more than anyone else!" he said defensively

Rheene snorted. "Not saying much there," he said quietly. The small white horse looked up at Owen. "But we *could* just take Molly and then come right back. The Tree said it might know more the next time we went to visit. It wouldn't take long."

Owen nodded and swished his tail. "Make it quick," the Centaur said.

Molly slid down off Owen's back as Rheene and Gossamer flew up to eye level. She smiled at Lorania and reached out to touch the hooves dangling in front of her.

"This should be a *blast*," Molly said to the nymph, rolling her eyes. And then she and the Wequen vanished.

Chapter Ten

Once again, Molly stood before the Tree of Knowledge. Rheene and Gossamer flew to the ground and stood beside her, looking up at the Tree's massive trunk.

"You have returned. Did you find Mother Nature?" the Tree asked.

Molly stepped forward with her hands on her hips. The Tree of Knowledge was still uninformed, and she had lost her patience. "It's gotten *more* complicated. Chaos is *everywhere* and *no one* knows where Mother Nature is!" she said, venting some of her frustration. "There are some cool things here away from Earth, but there's a lot of crappy stuff. A lot!" She thought of the nymphs being crushed by falling trees when Chaos had struck the first time, and the hand she'd seen sticking out from under a large chunk of stone back in the city the second time Chaos had appeared. "People are dying!" she shouted, flinging her hands out at her sides. "Chaos seems to be following us! I think Mother Nature has been captured, and I don't know how much time we have until Chaos destroys *everything!*"

Rheene and Gossamer were looking up at her in admiration.

"Couldn't have put it better myself," Rheene said to Molly with a nod of respect.

"You may be right," the Tree of Knowledge admitted. "Some have come to me with questions similar to yours since you left me last."

Molly leaned forward, waiting for the Tree to say more. "And?" she asked forcefully after a few seconds.

"I had not heard about Chaos," the Tree said, sounding as though it didn't believe her.

Molly reached back and touched the dried blood on the back of her left arm. "Well, it's ripping up the land, along with the crazy weather. Chaos is out there, destroying everything it touches! We were *hoping* you could help us get a lead. *Anything* to get us closer to finding Mother Nature!"

The Tree shook its branches and then was still, as if asleep.

Rheene stamped a hoof and shook his head. "Looks like that's it," he said. "About as much help as we got last time."

"It was worth a try," Gossamer said sheepishly. "Usually we get clearer answers."

Rheene nodded. "Usually," he said. "It's like he's confused and can't focus, or stay awake."

Molly was about to shout at the Tree to try and wake it when the winds suddenly kicked up.

"I'm…cold…" the Tree said slowly. "So…tired…"

Then its branches drooped and it looked even more like it was asleep. The Tree's green leaves looked dull and slightly wilted. Molly almost felt sorry for it.

She let out a frustrated sigh. "I guess we head back to the Gate

Keeper," she said.

The two small horses flew up without saying anything and Molly reached out and touched them.

"So?" the Gate Keeper asked as they appeared in his Hall. "What did the Tree say?"

"More rubbish," Molly said, waving her hand angrily. "It's like he's on drugs or something. No help – at all!"

"Not like usual," Gossamer said, still feeling a little defensive. "More proof that things are pretty messed up."

Molly dropped herself into one of the cushioned chairs, careful to keep from sitting on her pouches. She noted that her glasses were still gone. At least her clothes were still on, and comfortable, too. "We gotta find a place to start," she said. "Right now."

"That is why I have come," a deep voice said from behind her.

Molly twisted her head around at the sound of the vaguely familiar voice. The Cyclops was standing beside Owen. She hadn't even bothered to look in that direction when she arrived.

"I had a vision," the Cyclops said, his one eye staring at Molly. "I know where Mother Nature is."

Molly stood and leaned toward him, her hands on the back of the chair. "Finally! Where is she?!"

The Cyclops did not blink. "It was not a…positive vision," he said carefully. "I saw her, and it was only moments ago. Great peril surrounds her. Devastation and horrors."

The Gate Keeper stepped up beside the Cyclops and waved a hand at him as he spoke to Molly. "He's saying that there's more danger out there than just Chaos. However, I know where you have to start, and we can finally get you on track to find her – immediately!"

Owen walked over to Molly and she looked up at the nymph on his back. Lorania was looking back at Molly with terrified eyes. It looked as though Lorania had heard the vision that the Cyclops had had and was shaken up by it.

Oh, great! More bad news! Molly thought, mentally rolling her eyes. *I don't care to hear it. We're going, and I'm getting this crystal sphere into Mother Nature's hands!*

The Gate Keeper began to sing. The gateway in the Hall shimmered. The Realm that lay beyond was dark, and from it emerged a stench that churned Molly's stomach.

"She's there?" Rheene asked skeptically.

Molly got up on Owen's back. She leaned forward and whispered in Lorania's ear. "I don't care what the Cyclops saw, or what he said. No one around here seems to really know anything anyway. We've survived Chaos twice. We got the sphere. And now we're going to find Mother Nature. When we do, she's going to get it all figured out. We just have to be brave." Only Owen was close enough to overhear what she told the nymph. Her words made him smile.

"They shall tell stories about us someday," Rheene said as he and his partner followed the Centaur over to the opening in the gateway.

"Yeah," Gossamer retorted, "about how five idiots ran around trying to do the impossible."

"Sometimes it takes an idiot to believe that things are going to work out," Molly added. "I don't care if people think I'm an idiot. We're going to do this!"

The two small horses gave her a quick glance. It was brief, but she saw that her words had encouraged them. She gave Lorania's waist a quick squeeze and the nymph responded with a brief squeeze on Molly's arm.

The Gate Keeper was smiling at Molly as he sang. She thought she saw a troubled look in his eyes, but refused to let it deter her. The Cyclops, standing beside the Gate Keeper, had a similar look in his eye, but without the charm of a smile.

Let them worry, she told herself. *You got Owen, Lorania, Rheene, and Gossamer. You got your wits, too. They don't know me. They don't know how badly I want Dad back, or how I don't make a promise I don't intend to keep.*

She turned around as Owen entered the dark Realm. It reeked. The stench was so pungent she wrinkled her nose in disgust. She almost gagged.

The Gate Keeper ended his song and the gateway closed. Only the Cyclops remained in the Hall. "I know what you saw," the Gate Keeper said to him. "The parts you didn't tell the Centaur and nymph. That girl from Earth is going to die. She's not going to be a Dream Walker, will she?"

"I must return," the Cyclops said quietly, not answering the question. "Take me home," he commanded.

Molly had to cover her nose. She doubted that she would get used to the terrible smell in this new Realm. There were plenty of farms in Littletown. New York State had more farmland than most people not from that region knew about. She knew that she could get used to the smell of animal droppings, but it took time. Here, she didn't know if that would be the case. Apparently, Owen's ability to keep them safe from some wind and rain didn't work on smells.

From the Centaur's back, she looked around at the land. It was hard to see clearly among all the shadows in the Realm. A dark orange-red sky loomed overhead. She could just make out a rocky, barren landscape.

The nymph covered her nose. "Death!" she said with a shudder. "This place smells like death!"

"Where are we?" Molly asked, doing her best to not breathe in too deeply.

Owen was looking around as he slowly walked away from the gate. "The Cyclops did not tell me, and I do not recognize it. I was not listening to the Gate Keeper's song, either. Before you returned the Cyclops said that there are beings attacking some places. Not just Chaos. Mother Nature had come here for refuge. In his vision, he saw that she was still here somewhere, and alive. He also said that it would be dangerous, but nothing more, even though I am certain that he left out some of the more unpleasant details. It was then when you came back with Rheene and Gossamer."

There was a rough path leading away from the white gateway arch and Owen followed it at a slow trot. In some places it looked like a stampede had ripped up the path. Gouges and long, thin, deep cuts were raked across much of the ground. In other spots it looked like an earthquake had toppled rocks and split open the ground. Owen was careful to stay on the path and navigate, straying as little as possible. They traveled that way for a few hours, with very little conversation, as their eyes grew more accustomed to the darkness.

As they crossed the rocky terrain, a large red moon rose, giving them a little more light to see by. Molly's eyes had adjusted well by then, but the putrid smell still lingered. She breathed as shallowly as she could while she took in the Realm's landscape. The ground was rippled, rising and falling like small hills. With almost no plant life (a few wilted trees and bushes were all she'd been able to make out) this place had the feel of a desert – an old, dead, forgotten one. The air was stagnant, the temperature moderate, and had not fluctuated in the few hours they had been traveling.

Another strange thing that Molly thought about was how little the gravity changed from one place to the next. She knew that gravity changed from planet to planet, from sun to sun, and moon to moon. Yet, everywhere she Traveled since setting out on her journey, the gravitational pull felt the same. She understood every language. Even her breathing had been normal, as if the air consistencies everywhere were similar. She assumed it was the watch, but that would make it an even more extraordinary item than she had assumed – like a spacesuit, universal translator, time manipulator, air regulator, and who knew what else, all rolled into a small golden clock necklace!

"How come gravity and air consistencies don't affect me, Owen?" she asked the Centaur. "How can Rheene and Gossamer, who are from a Realm – where I'm basically an energy projection – go to different

Worlds and be solid if they don't have a pocket watch like mine?"

The Centaur smiled. "You know a lot for someone so young," he said.

"Probably just who I am," Molly replied. "My dad encouraged me to think things out for myself."

"Wise man," Owen stated. "As for your questions, the ways one can Travel between Worlds and Realms in numerous – perhaps even infinite. You already have the ability to leave your World – in your dreams, something I am sure you have done many times. The pocket watch simply enhances your natural ability to Travel. There are many beings who cannot Travel at all, mostly from Worlds. The watch is a unique gift from the Keepers, to allow you to be here fully, and lets you take some of their power with you on your journey: to compensate for such things as oxygen levels and gravitational pulls. Also, most habitable Worlds that have evolved intelligent species are quite similar. The variances in breathable air and gravity from World to World are minimal."

"How about Lorania?" Molly asked. "How can she Travel with us without a pocket watch?"

"Beings from Realms are made of different materials," Owen explained. "Traveling is quite easy for us – especially from Realm to Realm. We have not yet gone to a World on this quest. If we do, perhaps Lorania would not be able to exist there, or perhaps she would only appear in spirit."

Molly yawned as she nodded. "I see," she said, finding it difficult to keep her eyes open. She was intrigued, but exhausted. Lorania seemed to be slumping a little bit in front of her as well.

"How about we stop for some rest?" she asked.

The others agreed and they stopped in one of the little valleys. Molly took a sip from her canteen and ate another one of the delicious squares from her pouch. She offered some to the others, but they politely refused.

Molly was lying down beside Lorania, fidgeting with the gold chain around her neck, and slowly tracing her thumb along the side of the pocket watch.

"Can I see your *time machine*?" Lorania asked awkwardly.

Molly smiled, took the watch off of her neck, and handed it to the nymph. She didn't consider whether it was something she had to be wearing for it to work. For a brief moment, she thought she'd made a horrible mistake and anticipated that she was going to vanish and be back in her bed at home. But removing the watch changed nothing. She breathed a sigh of relief and watched as Lorania turned the watch over with her fingers in the red moonlight.

The nymph tapped the button on the top and made a delighted sound as she watched the lid swing open. Her large eyes squinted in the dark to see the photo of Molly and her parents inside the lid. "Can you tell me how this memory got in the time machine?" she asked Molly with a look of confusion and amazement.

Molly leaned closer to the nymph, looking at the picture. "Well, we have a thing called a 'camera' where I come from. It copies things you can see using light and lenses. It imprints the image you see."

Lorania did not look as though she understood anything Molly had said. The nymph looked exhausted and even weaker than she had before they had entered the Realm, too. Molly was doing her best to stay quiet and explain what a camera did, even though she knew very little about how they really worked.

Rheene and Gossamer were curled up with each other, sound asleep. Owen stood guard, insisting that he would keep watch and that he needed very little sleep.

"I would like to have a time machine with a memory of my sisters in it," Lorania said sleepily. Her large eyes closed and her smile turned into a face torn with sorrow. "It's so hard to remember their faces," she whispered sadly. "I have forgotten what Naomi and Sasha looked like."

Molly's heart went out to the grieving nymph. She wondered if Lorania had a short memory, of if the recent trauma had affected the nymph more than the others.

"Losing people you love really sucks," Molly said, thinking of her father and missing her mother as well. "Hurts like crazy...for a long time."

"Time machine with memory," Lorania said, opening her eyes a little and handing the pocket watch back to Molly. "I don't think I'll ever understand time, or why machines are part of it." The nymph yawned and curled up, facing Molly.

By the time Molly had put the gold chain around her head and lay down again, the nymph appeared to be sleeping deeply.

"That was fast," Molly whispered.

"She's slowly dying," Owen said quietly. "She's away from the trees. She's lost much of her family. And without Mother Nature, all living things are going to weaken – nymphs more than most as they are directly attached to the land."

"Dying?" Molly whispered.

The Centaur was only a couple of yards away, looking down at Molly, his muscular arms crossed over his wide chest. He face looked like stone in the red light. Molly also thought that he looked a little worried.

"Get some rest," he said gently. "Let me take care of you, so that you can complete your mission."

"OK," she said softly. Molly reached out and put a hand on Lorania's shoulder. She took a deep breath and realized that the smell wasn't as bad – most likely she was getting used to it.

She closed her eyes and fell into an uneasy sleep in a matter of seconds.

"Get up, Molly!"

She grunted at the urgent whisper in her ear.

"Get up!" the voice repeated, even more urgently.

Molly opened her eyes. She was still lying on the ground. The sky was still that dark orange-red. Gossamer was standing beside her head, looking down at her with an agitated look on his face.

"What is it?" Molly asked, groggily remembering that she wasn't in bed and waking up for school. "Is it morning?"

"Sshh!" Gossamer chided. "Keep your voice down," he whispered.

"Why?" she asked, sitting up.

Gossamer backed up a couple of steps to give her room. "There's something moving around out there," he said, pointing a hoof to where Owen was crouched and peering at something in the distance. "Something alive! It's coming this way!"

Lorania and Rheene were up beside the Centaur already and Molly crawled as quietly as she could over to them. Gossamer was at her elbow as she peered over the edge of the small rise. She could make out a shape moving in the dark over the rocky terrain about two hundred yards away.

It must be big if I can see it this well from this far away! she thought. It was the first living thing she'd seen in this Realm.

"There's only one," Molly noted in a whisper. "Let's go over to it and see if it has seen Mother Nature."

"It could be dangerous!" Lorania said.

"Maybe," Owen said quietly. "You and Molly will ride. Hopefully, we can find out something that will help us."

As they approached the moving dark shape, Molly began to make out its features. It had arms, legs, a tail, and even wings. It was still moving toward them. "A dragon," she breathed. "Is it safe, Owen?" she asked. Even though she could see it clearly, they were still about a hundred yards away and she thought that would be enough distance for them to escape.

"It appears to be injured," Rheene whispered.

"It is," the Centaur said firmly. "We should be safe enough. I know many dragons."

That didn't surprise Molly one bit. She watched as the wounded dragon lumbered toward them. In a few seconds Owen closed the gap between them and the dragon was right in front of them. It was huge, way larger than the one they'd encountered at the stone city standing guard with the Giant. Deep gashes covered its body and it had been bleeding for some time. Some of the blood had dried. It stooped down, almost collapsing in front of them.

"What has happened?" Owen asked the wounded dragon with deep concern. "Are you alone here?"

Lorania jumped off the Centaur's back and ran over to the dragon. By the time she reached it, it was lying down. She put her hands on the dragon's belly and looked up at it as her eyes filled with tears.

The dragon breathed in ragged breaths and its reptilian eyes were half shut. "A battle…in the city," it stammered in a male voice. "Things… defeated us…took Mother Nature…went for…help," it managed to say in a weak but heavy voice.

"Who did this?" Lorania wept. "Was it Chaos?"

"Not Chaos," the dragon replied in a forced voice. "Creatures I…had never…seen before." He paused for a few seconds. His eyes closed and he slumped a little more. "Killers…had to flee…warn others…" the dragon trailed off and Lorania whimpered. This time when it spoke, it was barely a whisper and its arms fell to the rocky ground. "Save… her…" Blood trickled from dozens of cuts, some deep. The dragon breathed out once more and then was still.

Lorania fell to her knees, sobbing.

The others had come up behind her and Molly jumped down to stand next to the weeping nymph. She knelt down. "Mother Nature is here, in this Realm," she said to Lorania. "The dragon completed his mission, and so will we."

"What do you suppose could do that to a dragon?" Rheene asked Gossamer.

The light brown horse shook his head. "I hope we don't find out," he replied. "Chaos was enough."

The nymph stood up, her sobbing faded as she took Molly's hand. They both got back up on Owen's back.

"Mother Nature," Lorania whispered longingly.

"We must be close," the Centaur said. "He couldn't have gotten far with those wounds."

Owen was right. After heading out in the direction that the dragon had come from, where the path was leading them, they crested one of the small hills and before them stood a city. It was vast, making the stone city they had visited before look very small in comparison. Thousands of buildings reached up from behind a massive wall. Molly had never before seen or imagined a city of this magnitude and scale. They were still miles away from it, but she had to turn her head from side to side to take it all in from the horizon.

Owen moved quicker, turning his trot into a near run. The city wall grew taller as they approached. It stood fifty feet high. Small towers punctuated the wall every two hundred yards. There was no gate, just an open area in the wall outside the city where the path led up to.

No guards manned the walls. No one came out to greet them. Molly and Lorania got off Owen's back as he slowed down at the opening in the wall. There were guards, but they lay dead at the foot of the massive stone wall. They were the dark-skinned, human-like beings with feathered wings they'd seen in the stone city. The armor they wore was light, covering their heads and chests. But the armor had done them no good. Like the dragon they had just left behind, the guards had been sliced up. Large gashes covered their dead bodies. Some had had their arms, legs, wings, or heads, completely severed.

"All dead," Owen said gravely. "We must keep going. Mother Nature is here somewhere and the danger is even greater than ever with all the city buildings. Enemies could be hiding anywhere. Be alert as we go into the city."

Molly and Lorania returned to him, not wanting to be among the dead, and climbed back on without a word.

Rheene and Gossamer flew closer to the Centaur as they entered the massive city…

Chapter Eleven

As they passed through the opening in the city walls, Molly was surprised to find a large open area, about three football fields long, between the city walls and where the first line of buildings stood on the other side of the open area. There were stone-paved paths that meandered through what Molly thought was an outdoor art gallery, for it was too big to be a courtyard. There were large stone-carved fountains scattered among thousands of sculptures of all kinds – some of different beings, some of plants, a few depicting complex scenes, and some that were very abstract. The fountains were dry and many of the sculptures had been smashed. A few bodies, torn apart like the dragon on the path and the winged guards outside the wall, were scattered along the road that led to the first line of buildings. Molly did her best to look at the art and not at the dead.

"I *have* been here before," Owen said slowly as they entered the huge outdoor gallery. "This isn't just any city, this is Raflure! It was named after the ancient ones who built it at the dawn of time. We have been in the Realm of Timeless Wisdom since we left the Gate Keeper's Hall! Only, it feels…*sick* now. That is why I did not recognize it before – it has changed drastically."

"Raflure?" Rheene asked the Centaur. "I've heard of Raflure before. Isn't this the biggest city in the Realm?"

"The biggest, and the center of most of the Realm's commerce," Owen said, surveying the courtyard with narrowed eyes. "To see it decimated is heartbreaking…and unnerving."

The Centaur sounded as if he were about to break down into tears. His voice was strained and the anguish was easy to hear. Molly could feel his tail swishing against her back. She was flat out terrified now. Between Chaos being able to strike at any moment and knowing that creatures were going around killing dragons, guards, and anyone else they encountered, she didn't feel as safe with her companions as she had a short while ago. The likelyhood that Mother Nature might be among those creatures, Lorania growing weaker, the Realm being dark and foreboding, and having to pass by the bodies of dead, made her wonder if she would be able to keep her nerve.

"Spooky," Gossamer commented. "It's so *quiet*," the light brown horse said in a hushed voice. "This place gives me the creeps, even though I've been edgy since we started."

Molly agreed with him, but didn't want to say so. She felt as if getting to Mother Nature alive with her little posse rested on her shoulders and she was going to supply as much moral support as she could find within herself – and not give in to her growing fear.

The first building they came to was small and run down. They didn't see anyone alive, or hear any sounds of the living as they entered the first row of buildings. There were dead bodies here as well, as if a large battle had been fought, but whatever had attacked the beings here had not left any dead behind...unless, Molly wondered, the beings had attacked themselves. However, the Cyclops had told them that it was a specific group of beings that were going around attacking places like Raflure, and she didn't think it likely the beings here had turned on each other.

There was a loud clatter behind them and Molly tensed in fear. Lorania cried out softly as they all turned toward where the sound had come from.

"What is it?" the nymph whispered to Owen.

"I don't see anything," Rheene said, flying a little closer to the Centaur.

"Just some falling rubble," Gossamer said hopefully.

They all looked and waited anxiously for a few seconds, but it was still and no more sounds came.

"Perhaps you are right," Owen said to Gossamer. "Keep moving. And stay on alert."

Molly breathed a sigh of relief as they turned and headed back deeper into Raflure. The city still frightened her, even though the lit lampposts lining the city streets gave them more light to see by. There were even more dead lying in the streets the further they went into the city. And it wasn't just the bodies that were sliced up. Large slashes and cuts were in the buildings, streets, lampposts, and other small structures everywhere: as though a giant rotating set of swords had mowed everything down.

Lorania shuddered. "Why have we only seen the dead?" she asked in a drained voice. "Did they kill *everyone* here?"

Owen didn't answer, but his trot became a gallop. The small flying horses flapped their wings faster to keep up. They were staying close to the Centaur, looking around with wide, watchful, eyes.

"So," Molly said, looking up at a tall building that rose hundreds of stories up into the dark orange-red sky, "how do we find Mother Nature here?"

"We follow the signs," Owen answered.

"So, you know where you're going?" she asked him.

"The Cyclops said she was here," Owen explained to her. "The dragon confirmed it, and we have seen the carnage left behind by the beings responsible for the killings he spoke of. If these destructive beings still have Mother Nature, as is suspected, then we follow the trail they have left for us."

"What if there's, like, hundreds of them when we get there? Or, thousands?" Molly asked, realizing that they could be heading closer to certain death. "As Lorania said, we haven't seen many survivors. And the only one we did see, died right after we met him. Doesn't look very promising."

"That's what we're here for!" Rheene said. "Gossamer and I can teleport all of us right next to Mother Nature when we find her. Or to a safe place if she's not reachable," he added, tilting his head as he thought about the different situations they could find themselves in. "Or if it's too dangerous," he finished nervously.

"Gotcha," Molly said.

The Centaur glanced back at Molly. He was smiling: albeit a grim one. "What do you think I have spent my time doing since I was created shortly after the Worlds and Realms came into existence? Organizing picnics and posing for artists?"

The absurdity of it made Molly laugh. She had a distinct image of him posing on cushions for a painter. But he was right. The Centaur, in spite of him being shaken by Chaos and faced with the unknown, had been leading them like a military commander since they'd met. Of course he had been doing things like this for (what Molly assumed was) billions of years. Owen was simply doing what was he was created to do. It didn't take away all of her fears, but it was a good reminder that she was with companions who were doing what they do best. Owen was leading a dangerous mission. Rheene and Gossamer were aiding them, ready to teleport them to the next stage when called upon, and Lorania was seeking Mother Nature for simple survival. Molly was no different, really. She had always been driven. She ran long distance for track, and didn't give up on things she'd set her mind to. They may be the only five living things in a city of the dead where an evil army may be waiting to ambush them, or where Chaos might strike, but they were still a force to be reckoned with.

Molly smiled. She looked back up at the tall buildings. She hadn't expected to find structures like this here, after seeing stone structures everywhere else. But these skyscrapers could have been pulled from any city back on Earth. Whether or not they were made of steel and concrete, she couldn't tell. This section of the city almost felt like being in a city on Earth – but the orange-red sky and the dead bodies of beings that were clearly not from Earth kept her from feeling at home here.

"This part of Raflure is really different from the open art gallery place inside the walls and that first section of buildings we went through," she said, hoping to keep her mind off of the horrible carnage around them and what could be waiting for them when they got to Mother Nature. "Is it like this through the whole city?" she asked, keeping her gaze turned upward as Owen trotted around a small pile of bodies.

"We are still in the outer rings," the Centaur replied, "far from the center. The city was built around the dragon section, at the heart of Raflure, where the king resides. The last I knew, Harnk was on the throne. Anyway, in that center part of the city, the buildings are quite large – some even larger than the ones here," Owen explained, sounding glad to be talking about the details of the city and its history. "Concentric circles were built for the different beings in the Realm around the center over time," he continued. "Eventually, after a few million years of construction, it was decided that the city was large enough and the dragon king, Jankula, ordered the outdoor sculpture exhibition to be installed and the outer wall to be built, to make sure the construction would not continue. There is no official capital city in the Realm of Timeless Wisdom, but if there were, Raflure would be it – as the laws of the Realm are made here, and the dragon who sits on the throne is responsible for much that happens."

"If the dragon we met was from the center, do we have to go all the way there to find Mother Nature?" the nymph asked, sounding a worried.

"Most likely," Owen replied.

"I can feel her," Lorania whispered. "She is weak, like me...I hope Mother Nature is not gravely wounded."

Molly lifted a hand and put in on the nymph's shoulder. Lorania felt frail and small. "We'll make it in time," Molly reassured the nymph.

"Or die trying," Gossamer added, sounding both heroic and sarcastic.

They didn't talk for a little while after that.

The next section of the city was quite different. It was easy to see how unique the different rings of Raflure were. The doors were taller in this part, but the buildings themselves were shorter. Molly didn't see any building over five stories tall.

Giants, like the one they had seen in the other city, lay dead here. That explained the taller doors.

Lorania whimpered. Molly hugged the nymph a little tighter and whispered, "Hold on, Lorania."

Suddenly, a figure darted out from the shadows of a building. Molly hadn't even noticed it before it stepped out, despite it being a mere ten yards away, and she jumped, startled by the sudden movement.

"Dork!" she whispered angrily at herself.

Owen and the flying horses stopped as the figure stepped in front of them, hunched forward as if ready to attack. "Who are you?" the hunched figure asked in a clear, female voice.

"A Giant!" Molly said aloud, recognizing what the figure was.

"You are *not* a Giant," the female Giant said, still leaning toward them in a menacing stance. "Answer my question. Who are you?"

"I think you *know* who I am," Owen replied. "We are on a mission to find Mother Nature," he said.

Molly was a little surprised at how quickly Owen got to the point, as if he knew he could take the Giant if she attacked, or as if he didn't care who knew who they were and what they were doing.

The Giant took a few steps closer, straightening up a little, revealing her true height. "Is *that* what this is all about?" she asked cautiously.

"Yep," Molly said, following Owen's lead. "Something's happened to Mother Nature."

She could see the Giant clearly now that she was closer, and standing up in the light. The Giant's dark blue eyes were sharp and intelligent, her black hair cut short. She wore leather clothing that was skin tight, although it was cut up and ragged in a few places, and her thick, dark brown leather boots were scuffed quite badly as well. Molly was pretty sure that the Giant had been in a fight, or escaped from a recent disaster.

Rheene and Gossamer flew to the ground, standing a little behind Owen for protection – and to rest their wings.

"You aren't discouraged by what you've already seen?" the Giant asked. "Do you think you'll be safe going further in?"

"The alternative is not much of a choice at all," Owen replied, almost harshly. "If we do not get to Mother Nature soon, Chaos may put an end to us all. Almost makes our decision for us."

The Giant relaxed even more and casually walked right up to them, striding like a cat: deliberate and with grace. "Then I will go with you," she said, looking at each of them in turn. Her gaze held a little longer on Molly, and the golden pocket watch she wore. "You are the first living things I have seen in two days...or what I *think* has been two days," she said, sounding relieved. "I hope you will have me."

"Are you sure?" Lorania asked.

The Giant nodded. "If what you say is true, and it makes sense to me, then I would rather be with you."

"Wise," Owen said. "Have you seen anything that could aid us?"

"Nothing I can think of," the Giant replied. "I arrived after the carnage had been done and have been wandering the last two days, searching for any sign of life. I overheard you talking and made my way here."

"You look like you saw some action," Molly said, pointing at the Giant's scuffed boots and tattered pants. "Was it Chaos?"

The Giant nodded slowly as if considering Molly's question. "Black spheres that ate the land and devoured the sea," she stated in a cold voice. "So it *is* Chaos, as I suspected. I haven't seen it here, though. This is the work of mad soldiers," she said with a graceful gesture at a pile of dead Giants. "Soldiers who don't seem to leave behind their dead." She looked at the bodies in anguish. "We are not easily killed," the Giant said angrily. "Either this is the work of a massive army, or killers with superior skills."

"You'll probably find out if you join us," Rheene quipped.

The Giant turned to look at the small white flying horse. "What will you do when you find Mother Nature?" she asked.

"I have a new crystal sphere for her," Molly cut in. "She'll get her powers back as soon as I get it to her. That's why we're trying to get to her."

The Giant smiled. She looked almost hopeful. "May I see it?"

"Owen?" Molly asked. "Do you think I should get it out here?"

The Centaur nodded and said, "Show her, and then we can be on our way."

Molly dug the misty sphere out and held it up for the Giant to see. "This is it," Molly said.

"Thank you," the Giant said. "I am Mesna, and honored to join you."

"Molly," said Molly as she put the sphere away.

The others said their names in greeting: all but Owen.

With that done, Owen began to trot down the road again, heading for the center of the city. Mesna jogged beside him, her long, lean legs striding elegantly. She ran easily and moved around obstructions in the street without pause. Rheene and Gossamer flew on the other side of the Centaur, having to work a little harder than the Giant to keep up.

They passed through the Giant's section of the city without seeing another living thing. The next part of Raflure was completely devastated. The buildings were toppled and the streets were torn up. Fallen stones covered some of the dead. Molly could see arms and legs sticking out from under the stones.

"Maybe I spoke too soon," Owen said as they began to make their way around the large chunks of debris. "Explosives could have done this. Maybe even sorcery. It seems more likely that this was done by Chaos, though. Sorcerers with this kind of power are rare."

"If we're sure we just need to get the center of the city, why don't we just teleport there?" Gossamer asked. "It doesn't look like we'll be running into many living things here, and it could take days to get through spots like this!"

"Why didn't we do that right when we got here?" Lorania asked.

Molly had thought something similar – just teleporting directly to Mother Nature after they had met the dragon. But she had no idea how to get around in the Worlds and Realms, and she'd been hoping that they would find Mother Nature before they'd gone very far.

"With so little to go on, I was following the trail to assess the situation," Owen replied. "We do not know exactly where Mother Nature is, or if we are walking into a trap," he said matter-of-factly. "We also do not know what we are up against, and I was hoping to discover more clues as to what we will be facing when we get to Mother Nature. However, I agree that this is getting tiresome, so, yes, we can teleport. Be on guard. We could be heading into a trap and end up directly in the midst of an army."

"You don't have to be concerned about that!" Rheene said. "One sign of trouble, and we're right back here!"

"I'm glad you found *me*," Mesna said. "*Before* you tried this."

Molly couldn't tell if the Giant was joking or not, but Mesna seemed sincere. The Giant reached out and put a hand on Owen's side, as if she'd been teleported by Wequen before.

"Ready?" Gossamer asked, looking down at them as he hovered over the Centaur's head.

Yep!" Molly said, holding tight to Lorania.

Owen reached up and touched the horses' hooves.

Nothing happened.

Owen took his hands away, and then tried again.

They did not teleport.

"Why isn't it working?" Molly asked. "Are there too many of us?"

"It doesn't work that way," said Rheene. "We've teleported groups before – large beings, too, like Centaurs and dragons."

"It's like our ability doesn't work here," Gossamer said in disbelief. "As if the magic in the air has died just like everything else!"

"So, what do we do now?" Molly asked, a little disheartened by them not being able to skip right to the end. She had started to get her hopes up.

"We keep going," Owen answered. "As we have been."

"If we're to keep going on foot," Mesna said to Molly as she took her hand off Owen, "I'd like something to eat. You don't happen to have anything in one of your pouches, do you?"

"Sure do!" Molly said, handing the pouch and canteen to the Giant. She watched as Mesna carefully fished out one of the squares with her Giant's fingers. The Giant was more than twice Molly's size. The small square looked amusingly small in Mesna's fingers. She tossed the piece into her mouth.

"It's delicious!" the Giant said. "Is the liquid as exquisite?"

"Oh, yeah," said Molly.

"Wonderful," Mesna agreed after a sip. "Thank you." She handed the pouch and canteen back to Molly.

This time, when Molly offered food and drink, the others had some, too – including Owen. Lorania seemed to come to life a little more after she had a drink from the canteen. Rheene and Gossamer also seemed to look healthier after they had nibbled on the juicy food squares.

They set off, a little discouraged by Rheene and Gossamer losing their ability to teleport, but just as determined to get to Mother Nature.

Owen and Mesna walked in silence. Rheene and Gossamer trotted, galloped, hopped, and flew to avoid large chunks of stone and lifeless bodies as they followed.

They passed through a few more rings of the city over the next hours.

Molly's sense of time was off and she guessed that it could have taken them as little as a few hours, or as long as an entire day. They saw carnage everywhere, but they did not encounter Chaos or any of the beings that had caused the death and destruction.

The sheer amount of devastation wore on them. It seemed as though every building was a sepulcher and every ringed section of Raflure was its own unique graveyard.

As a red moon began to rise in the orange-red sky, they decided to stop for rest.

"Over here," Mesna said, pointing to a domed building that looked to be in good condition.

There were two dead creatures in front of the building and the group moved around them to get inside. They were different than any of the other dead they had seen since they had been in Raflure. The creatures had two short legs with small feet and long, blade-like toenails. They had thin, muscular arms and long fingers with thick knuckles. They had abnormally long and sharp fingernails: almost like small swords sticking out from the ends of the fingers. Their torsos were thick at the shoulders and thin at the waist. They had grotesque faces with small ears, no noses, and two elongated, lifeless white eyes with small black pupils. Half of their face consisted of their mouths, which were filled with dozens of disjointed, razor-sharp teeth. Coarse brown hair protruded from their thick, lumpy skin. They stank worse than anything else in the city.

"I have never seen these...*creatures* before," Owen said. "But they are responsible for this."

"Those are the things that killed everybody?" Molly asked, covering her nose. Even though the whole Realm had stunk, these things were making her eyes water and her stomach clench. It was like the concentrated smell of a skunk mixed with ammonia.

"I've never seen the like before," Mesna said.

"Let's find another place to stay!" Molly said, gagging.

They moved further down the street to a similar building that was still intact and went in. Inside, the place was well-furnished and they found places to rest.

Lorania wiped tears from her eyes.

Molly looked at the nymph sympathetically and put an arm around the nymph. "It's gotten to me, too," she said. "It's…overwhelming."

Owen was standing in the center of the room with his arms crossed over his chest and his tail swishing even more than usual. "I have fought in countless battles, many wars," he said gravely. "Yet never have I seen anything like this. Whatever those creatures were out there, they must number in the *millions* to wipe out a city like Raflure."

"I can fight," Mesna said. "Even if to just give you an extra moment to get to Mother Nature," she added, looking at Molly.

"It may come to that," the Centaur said.

Molly watched Owen. He looked tired, for once. Maybe not as tired as she was, or as drained as Lorania, but he was clearly in need of this break.

"I just want this to be over with," Rheene said as he yawned. "Being professional is hard work."

Gossamer was nuzzled up to him, already dozing off.

"The dragon we met on the road here," Owen said, thinking out loud.

"Maybe it killed those two strange creatures out in the street. That would explain why they were left behind and not eaten like the others."

"Could be," Mesna agreed. "Maybe there are other factors that we have yet to uncover. I have doubts about those creatures acting on their own accord. They don't seem like beings with much capacity for thought, or planning."

Mesna was lying down with her head propped up so that she could see out of the window facing the road. Owen went over to the Giant as they engaged in a conversation about what could be motivating the stinky creatures, and if it had something to do with the return of Chaos.

Molly was beat and not interested in their conversation. Now that she was lying beside the two small horses and the nymph, her eyes were closing on their own. A moment later, Molly fell asleep.

Chapter Twelve

Molly woke in near darkness. There was movement around her. Owen was standing by the window looking out at the street and Mesna was going through some of the items in the large room they had stopped to rest in. It took her a moment to remember where she was and what she was doing. She found it odd that she did not dream while she here. If she was dreaming to be here, then maybe that was all the dreaming she could do.

"Nothing," Mesna said, setting down one of the many books she had been flipping through.

"It was fast," Owen said, still looking out of the window. "They must have swept through before an alarm could be raised. I have seen a few dead dragons, but they fly about so freely, it amazes me that those flightless, clawed creatures could get at them in the sky."

"The ones that stink like crazy?" Molly asked groggily.

"Yes," Owen replied.

The Giant bent down closer to Molly and smiled. "He and I spoke while you slept."

"The whole time?" Molly asked.

Mesna shook her head. "No. I needed some rest as much as he. But this whole situation is perplexing. So many dead," the Giant said sadly, shaking her head slowly. Her short black hair barely moved. "This feels precise, like a planned invasion. It's as if they knew when the guard changed at the gate and when the city's inhabitants would be at their most vulnerable."

"Does it change anything?" Gossamer asked, still lying on his side. He stretched his wings wide, brushing Rheene across the face, and yawned.

"No," Owen said. "Not right now."

"Time to go, then?" Rheene asked as he gave Gossamer an annoyed look.

"Yes, little one," Mesna said kindly. "You two are brave, to be going into this without your ability to teleport."

"Well, it isn't like we can just *leave*," Gossamer said, standing up. "Going back without you is less appealing than facing those stink monsters with you."

Molly smiled at Gossamer's sarcasm and honesty.

She felt filthy and wanted to take a shower, but knew that it might be a while before that was possible. It was mindboggling to think about being in a dream (or astral projection) so long, and in such a real way, that she needed to clean up from the extended stay.

She grabbed a snack, shared with the others, and then they went back out to the road to continue the trek to the center of Raflure.

It was silent, the sky still a dark orange-red, and every step that hit the stone road echoed. More dead littered the streets. Molly was starting to get used to seeing them, even though it was wearing her down. And she knew that she wasn't the only one.

"So, Rheene," Molly said in an attempt to sidetrack their thoughts as they moved through the gloomy city, "where do you guys come from?"

"Gossamer and I were born in a Realm where there is nothing but fields of wheat and sugar cane," the small flying white horse said. "After being in this place, it seems like paradise."

"You're not kidding," Gossamer said. "There's more than just wheat and sugar cane there. Lots of bugs, too."

"You know what I mean," Rheene said to Molly. "We're born there and grow up a bit before we're ready to go out on excursions like these. I guess we get to go back there when our teleporting days are over. We're all too young right now to know for sure, since none of us are more than a few years old, but it seems like a good way to live out one's last days."

"So every Wequen can teleport?" Molly asked, enjoying the conversation with her two adorable companions.

"Not at birth, but after a couple of years," Rheene replied. "We've been told that we'll lose our teleporting ability in our advanced years." He paused for a moment to think. "We're not *old* yet, are we, Gossamer?"

Owen let out one short, sharp laugh. "You are not old," the Centaur said. "Not even close. This part of The Realm of Timeless Wisdom is in some sort of malady and it is draining energy from all of us. I rarely rest, or eat, and yet here I find it necessary. Your inability to teleport has nothing to do with your age."

"You don't have to make it sound like we're colts," Gossamer said defensively, sounding a little hurt.

"Well…" Owen said, trailing off as though he didn't intend to finish.

Molly thought he was making a joke. It was good hear him join in the banter. She looked over at Mesna. The Giant was striding along fluidly as Owen trotted. "What about Giants?" Molly asked. "What kind of stuff do you do?"

Mesna gave Molly a curious look. "Is this the first time you've been away from your World?" the Giant asked.

"The first time I know of," Molly answered. She remembered Father Time saying that she'd never been 'here' before as strongly as she was now. Maybe she'd peeked through some kind of 'dream window' into other Worlds, or Realms, before. Her companions were giving her answers, but it was a lot of new information and she was still focused on getting to Mother Nature – so she could be with her father again.

Molly looked up at Mesna. There was more than just intelligence in the Giant's face. There was wisdom. However, there was a strong curiosity, too. And underneath them, there was something dangerous. Something Molly hadn't seen before.

Mesna just pursed her lips and went on. "With our size, strength, and minds for building, we have constructed many things throughout the Worlds and Realms. Have you seen Falib? The city of reflected light?" she asked.

Molly shook her head.

"I've heard about it," Gossamer said.

"I've seen it!" Lorania said, sounding cheerful for the first time. "Many nymphs live outside the city, and Mother Nature took my sisters and I there to meet with them," she explained, her eyes distant as she remembered. "It is a beautiful city," she commented. "For a city," she added. "I remember the dancing the most."

There was something special about the small group of companions Molly was with. Something that was bonding, powerful, and she began to think of them as 'Molly's Posse.'

"How about you, Owen?" Molly asked the Centaur. "Have you been to Falib?"

"Often," he replied. "The Centaurs visit Falib frequently, for many reasons. The Prophetess lives there, at the great library. The city of reflected light is more than just a beautiful work of art, it is a place of knowledge and learning."

"What's it look like?" Molly asked Mesna. "Is it made of mirrors or something?"

"Reflective surfaces," the Giant answered. "Metals, glass, even pools of water in some places. The angles of many structures are measured and cut to maximize the effect, so not many buildings are at square angles. It is never dark in Falib."

"Sounds pretty," Molly said. "Maybe I'll get to see it someday."

They passed into the next ring of the city. Here, the buildings were low to the ground and very simply made, almost like huts and cabins. They were made of wood, but had color-tinted windows and large gemstones on the doors. Had it been lighter, Molly was sure that it would have looked magical. The road itself changed a little here – it was made of cobblestones.

Dead beings lay everywhere. They had heads that looked like eagles, large feathered wings, cat-like bodies, and were about the same size as Owen. Molly recognized them as Griffins. Their dried blood covered the stones.

Molly realized something strange as she looked around. "Where are all the flies?" she asked out loud, recalling Gossamer's comment about the Wequen home Realm having lots of bugs.

"Flies? Those pesky things?" Gossamer asked, sounding disgusted. "Ugh." He shook his mane. "*Horseflies…*" The small light brown horse stuck out his tongue. "You know how bad it is for horses, and Centaurs, when you have flies named after you!"

"I noticed as well," Owen said to Molly over his shoulder. "My guess is that this part of the Realm is even too sick for them. Nothing has begun to decay for days, only death has taken place."

Molly didn't like the sound of that. The trip through Raflure was gross and depressing enough. She didn't care to know more about death and decay and dropped it. She was more interested in Falib, the city of reflected light, and what Mesna could tell her about libraries. Books were not just a hobby for her, more like a necessity.

"Have you ever built a library?" she asked the Giant.

"A few," Mesna replied. "For the most part, I journey to different Realms to see their unique sights. I have been to a couple of Worlds, but they don't have the history that the Realms do. Worlds had to evolve, where Realms came into being ready to go. Most of the history is from here, the Realm of Timeless Wisdom, since this is where it all started. Falib has many books on it, although there are some impressive libraries here in Raflure. Buildings themselves aren't something I find as interesting as the history around them, and in them. My plan is to write an all-encompassing compilation of the histories of all cities – and those who built them. There are some in the archives at Falib, but nothing that really tells about the beings themselves and why they did what they did. Names, dates, and materials are in most volumes, and those bore me. I want to be out here, where history is happening."

"Well, history is happening right now!" Rheene said.

"You know it," Molly said. "We're going to save Mother Nature, and that's a big deal."

Mesna chuckled. "You're a spark," the Giant said. "I value that."

"Thanks," Molly said, smiling at the compliment.

No one spoke for a little while. They moved through the Griffins' section of Raflure. It was dark, silent, tense, and the stench was still everywhere. Molly wondered if one of those stinky creatures would jump out and attack them. But none did.

"This was a great city," Owen said sadly.

"It still is," Mesna countered. "Only, it's under a shadow now."

"Raflure is commerce and art." The Centaur said. "…a city of life and diversity…reduced to a cemetery."

They passed a building that had been gutted from the inside. A side wall was gone, along with the roof and a large section of the front wall.

"Chaos again," Mesna commented.

"You mentioned before that you saw it 'drink the sea,'" Owen said to the Giant. "What, exactly, did you see?"

"I was sailing, returning from a trip to visit the city of Kaslep, when the black bubbles rose up from beneath the sea," the Giant explained, locking eyes with the Centaur. "They did not rise like pockets of air. Instead, they swallowed the water as they moved through it, as if they were gaps in reality." Mesna glanced at Molly, and then at the golden chain and pocket watch around her neck. "Chaos opened holes in the sea, pulling our ship toward it in jolts and skips. If not for the captain's skill, we surely would have been devoured."

"Does Mother Nature really have the power to keep Chaos away with just her crystal sphere?" Molly asked, imagining how terrifying it would have been to be on that boat with Mesna.

"Not *just* the sphere," Owen corrected. "That is an extension of her power, to be able to see everywhere, to be able to go where she is needed. No," he stated firmly, "it is more about the Keeper being in serious danger than losing her sphere. With this illness here, it must be draining her energy as well. Maybe more so if there are other, unknown, factors."

"We'll get to her," Molly assured them.

It took them longer to cross this section of the city. Chaos had done significant damage and many buildings had toppled onto the road. After a couple hours, they took another break. Molly slept uneasily, but still did not dream.

When they started out again, it was slow at first, but they got through the places where Chaos had hit and then made excellent time. Owen and Mesna ran. Without the ability to teleport, Mesna cradled Rheene in one arm and Gossamer in the other. She could run fast and they moved closer to the center of Raflure at over forty miles an hour.

A short time later, there was commotion ahead of them as a few large stones fell onto the road. Owen and Mesna slowed down until they stood where the stones lay. Two figures were huddled against the building from where the stones had fallen.

"Come out," ordered Owen in a firm, kind voice.

The figures were silent and did not move. Mesna set Rheene and Gossamer down, ready to take action if it was needed.

"We will not harm you if you do not attack us," the Centaur assured the crouching figures. "Step out and show yourselves."

The two figures looked at each other and spoke in fast, sharp conversation. One of them shook its head and then stepped a few paces away from the other, closer to the road.

"I saw the horrors that befell the city," the figure said in a frightened voice.

Molly thought that the figure in the street looked somehow familiar, as if she'd seen it before. It was human-like, standing on two legs, and it had two long arms dangling at its sides. Its head was thrust forward, following the exaggerated curvature of its spine. The plain face looked haggard, and not very intelligent. Instead of hair it had small flaps of skin, or fins, running from just above the eyes to the back of its head. She didn't think it looked threatening at all.

"What did you see?" urged Owen.

The figure in the road shifted his feet awkwardly, wrung his hands, and swayed from side to side. "Terrible," he said in a deep, cracked voice. "Cutting, screaming…" He wrung his hands faster and harder. "They moved like a tidal wave…one great…" He stopped wringing his hands long enough to make a motion with an arm, demonstrating a downward sweep and crash. "So fast. Killing. Eating. Eating their own dead." The poor creature's words were punctuated with coughing as he spoke. "Mindless. Just stabbing…slicing. None were singled out. Every living thing…cut down." He coughed a little harder. "We were in a tower, sealed, but able to look down on the slaughter. The dragons tried to get them, but they…" he paused, blinked, and made a weak throwing gesture. "They *threw* each other at the flying dragons…and then they were gone."

His companion cautiously stepped out from behind the building and shuffled over to stand beside him. "We must make it to the gate," the being said in a feminine voice. "Away from..," she lowered her head and pointed down the road that led to the center of Raflure.

"Our path leads to the center," Owen stated. "We are going there with or without you."

"You will be killed," the male said, aghast.

Owen turned away from them and continued on, leaving the two lone figures standing in the middle of the road. Molly looked back over her shoulder a moment later and saw that the two pathetic creatures had gone.

'Molly's Posse' passed more buildings, and yet another new race of dead beings. These were squat beings with four stumpy legs and very round torsos. They had heads like seahorses and small fins instead of arms. There were pools and canals everywhere in this part of Raflure, over which were elegant bridges.

Molly found it deeply disturbing to look at the dead (and severed body parts) to determine which beings lived in which section of Raflure, but she couldn't help looking in spite of her sorrow and disgust.

It was easy to tell when they got to a different section of the enormous city. The buildings often gave obvious clues, like the large, tall doors in the Giant's section, or the waterways for the sea creatures in this part. Molly found that she couldn't help trying to figure out which type of being lived in each ringed section of Raflure. She was taking mental notes, giving herself more motivation to get the crystal sphere to Mother Nature before more terrible things like this could happen.

With just a small amount of debris, and not many dead in the road, they made great time. As they entered the next ringed section of the city, Owen spoke up.

"We are close," he said, slowing down a little. "Keep your eyes keen and your ears alert."

"One more section," Mesna said. "And then we'll be at the center."

Molly refused to look down at the dead in this part of the city. Even so, from the sides, she could see dead dragons, unicorns, Giants, fairies, those small bear-like beings she'd seen before, a couple that looked like a cross between ostriches and camels with three humps, long necks, two legs, and covered in thick fur. She could also see a Griffin, a few beings that looked almost human, and an insectoid that looked like a dragonfly with its slashed wings sticking straight up.

She grimaced and let her gaze stay upward. A tall tower rose far above everything else. She pointed to it. "That must be a mile high!" she exclaimed.

"The Tower of Raflure," Owen announced. "The precise center of the city."

In a few minutes, they passed through the section they were in. No one spoke, but they all watched and listened intently for any sign of life.

The buildings at the center of the city were made for dragons – and they were immense! Rounded towers stood tall, like pillars with cones at the top. While the Tower of Raflure was the tallest, all of the other towers in this part of the city were higher than any of the buildings in the previous section.

"There!" Owen said, pointing ahead of them.

Standing in front of one of the dragon towers was a figure dressed in dark rags, leaning on a scythe.

Molly looked at the figure in trepidation and wondered if this was going to be the end of her journey. "Death!" she whispered quietly to herself. "Are we too late?"

Chapter Thirteen

Molly slid off the Centaur's back. She pushed the two sacks and the canteen farther back on her shoulder, closer to her neck, pinning the straps to her sides with her arm, and then took a deep breath. Lorania reached out a hand from beside her and Molly took it as the nymph joined her. Mesna let go of Rheene and Gossamer and they flew over to Molly, Lorania, and Owen.

Death raised his head as 'Molly's Posse' approached.

"Why do you linger here?" Owen asked the Keeper.

"I am weary," Death replied softly. "The sheer numbers of the dead and dying has weakened me."

"No kidding," Gossamer said somberly.

"There is more energy to transfer than ever before in the history of the Worlds and Realms," Death stated wearily. "The burden is exhausting. To be in so many places at once has drained me, more than I ever could have anticipated..."

"There are *other* places like Raflure?" Molly asked, heartbroken.

"Many," Death affirmed. "It is taking a great effort for me to appear here physically...other cities are being decimated as we speak...millions dead…soon to be billions…perhaps trillions."

Lorania let out a whimper and visibly hunched forward as if a sack of stones had been placed around her delicate neck.

"Why can't the other Keepers help?" Molly asked. "Medusa looks like a bad ass, and Father Time could stop time for everyone but us, or something, right?"

"Medusa is the only one of us who takes action as a warrior," Death explained. "The rest of us are not much more than Keepers…although I can feel that Medusa has grown weaker…like all of us. She is not able to teleport here with this part of Realm drained of its energy and by the time she could arrive here by other means, it would most likely be too late!"

"I agree," Owen said in a firm voice, his tail swishing.

"If Medusa can't teleport here, how did you get here?" Molly asked.

"The dead override the power of teleportation," Death replied. "The energy of the recently deceased calls me in way beyond the standard means to teleport."

"What about Mother Nature?" Owen asked Death

"Yeah, where is she?" Molly asked, still determined to complete her task. She was looking at the blackness under Death's hood but could not see his face, not even a hint of a white skull, if that's what was truly there. His hands were bony, though not actually bone, and were not covered with skin.

"She is being held captive," Death said in a slightly stronger voice. "Deep underground…beneath the city."

"By the same foul creatures that are raiding the Worlds and Realms?" Mesna asked.

"They are called Neuos: beings from another Realm," replied Death. "Evolved, perhaps, or physically and mentally manipulated over time. I am not certain. They sought out Mother Nature first, to weaken us all – every living thing. The energy is leaving…as life fades. Neuos thrive on it, as they are creatures of destruction, seeds of Chaos." He stood and began to walk towards the Tower of Raflure. "Follow me."

"If they can wipe out a city like this, what will we be able to do against them?" Owen asked.

Suddenly, Death began to flicker, as if he was fading from sight. He paused for a couple of seconds until his full form regained its solidity. His bony fingers gripped his scythe tightly. "Most of them are gone, off to destroy another city," he answered the Centaur. "You should be able to fight off the ones between you and her…" He flickered again. "I grow weaker…hurry!"

They wound their way through the city streets, passing beside dozens of dead dragons. Molly was glad their journey was almost at an end. She had enjoyed having her companions by her side, but the trek through Raflure had been agonizingly depressing and had worn them down.

When they reached the Tower of Raflure, Death stopped. "There is a passageway that leads under the Tower, to many chambers. The lowest is where Mother Nature is…" He flickered again, this time disappearing completely for a couple of seconds. "Hurry!" He leaned against his scythe for support. His hooded, invisible face turned towards Molly. "Become a Dream Walker," he said. "You have what it takes. I can feel it, sense it radiating from you..." He flickered once more. "But you must hurry!" He flickered again, and then vanished completely.

Molly felt an overwhelming sense of urgency. The entire time she'd been on her journey there was a desire to move quickly, to avoid Chaos, evade the erratic weather, and keep watch for the Neuos. But now it was a different kind of urgency. Death wasn't just trying to help them. Being in his presence, she got the strong impression that he was desperate and, even worse, afraid. As clichéd as it was, the fate of existence seemed to hang over 'Molly's Posse' and their search for Mother Nature.

Lorania looked on the edge of tears. Rheene and Gossamer looked scared out of their wits. Mesna and Owen, however, looked grim – like they were going into battle. Their hands where clenched in fists and their eyes were hard.

"Come on, Posse!" she said, looking at Rheene and Gossamer. "We're going to finish this." She reached out to squeeze Lorania's hand and gave Mesna and Owen her own grim smile of determination. "You are 'Molly's Posse' now and that means we're freakin' awesome! We're *doing* this – together!"

Molly walked up to the doors at the base of the Tower. The handles were too high for her to reach, but Mesna was already there, taking hold of the great handles in her strong hands. The Giant swung the doors open and they entered, leaving the dark orange-red sky behind them.

The entrance of the Tower of Raflure was a wide corridor, lit with small fires burning in crevices at regular increments in the wall. There were weapons hanging on the walls, along with banners and pieces of art.

They moved down the corridor a short way until they came to a room. There were a few dead dragons there, but not much else.

"Over there!" Owen said, pointing to a large door in the far corner.

"That leads underground to the chambers."

"Have you been down there before?" Molly asked.

"No," Owen replied. "But I know the basic layout of the Tower. The other way leads to throne room, and the back way to the kitchens is that door on the other side of this room."

"We're professionals," Gossamer muttered to himself, but loud enough for the others to hear. "We're professionals."

"You're my friends," Molly said to him. "Come on."

They reached the door and Mesna once again stepped up to open it. Molly was glad to have the Giant with them. Owen was a large being, but Mesna was over four feet taller than him. It was as if Mesna joining 'Molly's Posse' was something predestined, as it made it easier to do things like open doors with handles ten feet off the ground.

On the other side of the door were large stairs leading down. Each step was about three feet tall. Rheene and Gossamer flew. Mesna stepped normally. Owen showed great agility by stepping down at a slight angle. Molly and Lorania had to jump down each step.

Flaming torches lines the walls of the stairwell. Some had gone out, but most were still burning. Owen reached out and plucked a bright one from the wall as they descended.

The walls were etched with scenes of battle. Men on dragons engaged in battle, set against a backdrop of burning towers. There was one that showed scary-looking water creatures attacking human-like beings with wide chests in an underwater confrontation. The human-like beings were bald, with wide nostrils, and were armed with spears. Molly was busy watching her footing as she dropped from step to step and didn't have time to stop and look at the beautiful artwork closely.

The first flight of stairs came to an end, where they entered into another large room with two doors – one on the left and one on the right.

"Which way?" Rheene asked.

"Not sure." The Centaur said. He pointed left. "Let's try that one and see if it leads down."

They went over to the door and Mesna opened it. It swung open smoothly and quietly on its hinges. They entered, Owen thrusting the large torch forward and as high as he could. Three dead dragons lay in the center of the room. There was another dead being among them. A large gash ran down the length of its torso. It was humanoid, naked, with dark brown skin that was covered in small bumps and coarse hair. It had long fingers with wickedly sharp long nails. The small head had small ears, no nose, and was misshapen. Its elongated white eyes were open, with small black dots of pupils. Its mouth was open as well, with long, jagged sharp teeth.

"Another Neuo," Owen said. "Like the two we found back in the city."

Molly plugged her nose. "Just one, but smells as bad as the other two," she said, breathing shallowly.

Rheene walked around the body and behind a fallen dragon. When he appeared on the other side he said, "Do you think it killed all three? They are so much larger than it is…"

Owen was looking over the scene carefully. "They killed it, as it killed them," the Centaur said. "A waste," he finished in disgust.

Suddenly, the ground began to shake and small pieces of cracked ceiling and wall fell to the floor. The sound grew louder, the shaking increased. Lorania held tight to Owen and Molly reached out a hand to help steady the nymph. A beam crashed to the floor, breaking apart and scattering bits of debris.

"Chaos," Owen said, speaking the thing they were all thinking of.

As suddenly as it had begun, the shaking stopped.

"Do we go back and try that other door?" Molly asked, her heart pounding beneath the golden pocket watch.

"We do," Owen replied.

They went back the way they had come and went through the door on the other side of the room. The room had fared worse than the one they had come from. The pillars on the sides of the room had fallen and the ceiling had caved in.

"Glad we tried the other one first," Gossamer commented. "Looks like Chaos did some rearranging here!"

"Back," Owen said, leading them back to the room with the three dead dragons and the dead Neuo.

"What door?" Mesna asked, ready to open the way.

"Wait!" Lorania said, stopping. The nymph was squinting, one hand over her chest and the other touching her temple. "I…I can *feel* her!" she said, almost swooning. "She is reaching out! She knows we're here."

"Mother Nature?" Molly asked hopefully.

The nymph nodded emphatically. "Oh, yes!" She pointed to the door on the left. "That way!"

The Giant took a few smooth strides to the door and flung it open. Again, it was a large stairway leading down. Owen, torch in hand, led the way.

Lorania seemed to grow stronger with every step. She jumped down them as easily as Molly and there was a hint of a smile on her lips. The stairway only had fifteen stairs. There was no room or doorway at the bottom. A long dirt passageway that sloped down at a slight angle was their only choice. With just the one way, Owen led on without hesitation. There were fewer torches down here, but their eyes had adjusted. It was a little smokier, too, but the ventilation system still seemed to be working well, even all the way down here. The earthy ceiling was still high enough for Mesna to walk without stooping in the tunnel, as if the area had been dug out recently but still with dragons in mind.

"She can feel the sphere," Lorania whispered. "They're calling to each other."

Molly was about to ask the nymph to explain the connection when Owen suddenly stopped. The Centaur put out his torch with his bare hand, and ordered them to be silent and step back against the wall. He pointed down the passageway. Molly hadn't noticed it a second ago, but there was a shadow moving down there, and not from the flickering flames.

Something was crawling along the side of the long passageway. It passed underneath one of the torches and Molly could see it clearly, about seventy-five yards away.

A Neuo! she thought, frightened at the sight of a living one. The gut-wrenching pungent smell it radiated hit her. The Neuo made its way closer to them as they huddled silently against the wall. The Neuo was sixty yards from them, then fifty. Forty.

With a surprising burst of speed, Owen leaped out from the wall and down the tunnel – right at the Neuo! It stopped, surprised. But in three seconds, the Centaur was on it. Molly was as surprised as the Neuo. She almost cried out after Owen in alarm, fearing for his safety, but she remembered the way that he had caught, and tossed aside, the falling tree in the forest like it had been a tiny sapling. She watched in amazement and horror as he took hold of the Neuo's arm and yanked it off the wall. The Neuo tried to swipe at the Centaur with its razor-sharp nails, but Owen was still using his momentum to swing the Neuo around, away from his body, and slammed it against the wall. Molly could hear the Neuo's bones break and a gross wet sound as it was crushed by Owen's sudden attack. Owen dropped the dead thing and then motioned for the rest of them to follow.

When they reached the scene of Owen's lightning-quick assault, Molly found that she couldn't help looking at the mashed body.

"Yeeew!" Rheene said softly, covering his nose with a wing. "It stinks worse than the other ones!"

"Keep your voices down and watch out for more," Owen said.

Gossamer was looking up at the Centaur with admiration. "An honor to see you in action, sir!" he said, careful to keep his voice down.

Owen didn't look pleased, only focused, determined.

"A true professional," Rheene added, glancing at his partner.

"One of those things killed three dragons," Gossamer whispered to Rheene in awe. "And he took it out with *one swing*."

Lorania was doing her best to ignore the dead Neuo and stay in contact with Mother Nature's energy. "She's weak, but still knows we're coming," she said to Owen.

He nodded and then looked at Mesna.

"Take the rear," he said to the Giant. He looked down at Molly. "Follow me. Not too close, in case more Neuos are in front of us. When we get to her, we'll need you ready. Get out the sphere."

He waited a moment while Molly pulled out the crystal sphere.

"Good," the Centaur said. "Now," he pointed at Rheene and Gossamer, "you follow beside her. Attack from above with your hooves if we are set upon."

"We're going to fight?" Rheene asked.

"If it is needed," Owen confirmed.

The small flying horses exchanged a look of doubt, but nodded to each other and flew up beside Molly. She felt a lump in her throat. They were willing to die for her. Not just Rheene and Gossamer, but Owen, Lorania, and Mesna, too.

"She's so close," the nymph said.

"Come on," Owen said, and cautiously continued down the sloping tunnel that led to Mother Nature.

Chapter Fourteen

The underground passageway came to an end. The Centaur, the two Wequen, the Giant, the nymph, and Molly looked up at the large door standing before them. Two dragons were carved on it, intertwined and facing each other. They had not seen another Neuo since the one that Owen had taken out, and it was quiet. Mesna stepped up from the rear and pointed silently at the door, giving Owen a questioning look.

The Centaur made a motion for the others to keep back and then nodded to the Giant. Owen crouched, ready to attack.

Mesna pushed the doors open a crack as silently as she could. She peered through the space between the doors. After a couple of seconds, she pushed them open a little more and gestured to Owen for him to follow. When the Centaur had a good look through the doorway, he motioned for the rest of them to follow him.

Molly stayed close behind him as they entered an immense room. It wasn't furnished, but the room had stone walls, half a dozen beam supports from which light was emanating, and a high ceiling – unlike the tunnel behind them. She thought it looked like an underground hanger – except that instead of airplanes, there were dead dragons lying all around. Dozens of them. The stench was worse here than in any other part of the city. Lorania collapsed, reaching out to brace herself as she hit the floor. Molly's stomach twisted as she knelt down bedside the nymph.

There was movement on the far side of the large room.

"Neuos!" Gossamer cried out in alarm. "They see us! They're coming this way!"

Owen turned to the Giant, said, "Take the ones that get by me," and then darted out to meet the oncoming Neuos.

Molly watched in terror as five Neuos rushed towards them. They ran swiftly, hunched forward, claws outstretched, and shrieked like banshees.

Lorania covered her ears and Rheene let out a gasp of horror.

"Stay behind me," Mesna ordered them, and then took a few steps forward, knees slightly bent, her hands in fists.

The room was two hundred and fifty yards long and the Neuos had covered half that distance in mere seconds. Owen was surprisingly fast and had nearly matched their speed. The lead Neuo came at him, swiping, and turning sideways. Owen evaded it, nimbly darting a couple of steps to avoid the deadly claws, and turning to kick it in the center of its chest with his hind legs. When he made contact with the lead Neuo, the smacking sound echoed in the massive room. It flew almost twenty yards, landing on one of the dead dragons. The Neuo was dead before it settled into a heap by the dragon's tail.

Two more Neuos came at him, giving Owen less than a second to recover and face them. The other two Neuos moved around him as they darted by. Ignoring them, he reached out as the one closest to him attacked. He caught the Neuo's muscular arms in his hands and jerked it in front of the other attacking Neuo. The attacking Neuo's claws tore through the Neuo he was using as a shield. Owen dropped the dead Neuo he'd used as a shield. He reached out and grabbed the other one by the sides of its misshapen head and twisted violently. The Neuo stopped shrieking, head drooping, as it fell dead beside the gored Neuo.

Molly had watched the Centaur in awe and fear. The three Neuos had died quickly by Owen's hands – and hooves. *No wonder he told Rheene and Gossamer to attack with their hooves!* she thought to herself. *Those things are lethal!*

But now only a few seconds separated the last two Neuos and herself. The Giant was in front of her, ready. Molly was surprised to find that Mesna was as fast as Owen. The Giant moved like a cheetah. She jumped, turning sideways, and kicked the Neuo coming at her into the other one. Both flew back. Owen was racing to assist her. He reached the kicked Neuos the same instant that Mesna did. He trampled one as Mesna ripped the arms off of the other. She came down on its head with her boot.

All five Neuos were dead. It had taken less than fifteen seconds. Molly realized that she had been holding her breath. She began to breathe again and looked up at Rheene and Gossamer. They looked back at her with wide eyes, astonished.

"Professionals?" Molly asked them, almost breathless.

"No joke," Rheene said.

"I heard about what Centaurs could do," Gossamer said, "but seeing it is a different thing! Who knew Giants were warriors?" he added. "They're not just architects and book worms, but proper professionals when it comes to taking out Neuos!"

"I'm glad I didn't see it," Lorania said weakly. "However, I'm feeling a little stronger. Thank you, Molly."

The nymph stood up with Molly's help. The Centaur and Giant had returned by the time Lorania was on her feet.

"Did I say that I was glad that you guys came along?" Molly asked them. "Because I'd be dead meat if you weren't with me."

The Giant smiled grimly. "I was meant to be here," she said.

Owen swished his tail and gave Molly a slight nod. "You are welcome," he said. "Shows how ill prepared the Creator is, to send you out to meet these things without an army," he said. "But, perhaps, it *was* meant to be this way." He looked down at the nymph. "Can you walk?"

Lorania nodded and rubbed her left arm with her right hand.

"Good," the Centaur said. "If we run into more Neuos, having you on my back will not do. Come on."

He led them to the other side of the immense room, to the only other door. It was smaller than the ones they had come in through. Mesna opened it like she had the other one – Owen crouched and ready, with the rest of 'Molly's Posse' behind him.

Mesna turned back to look at Owen. "Nothing. Too dark. We'll need light."

"Gossamer and I can go back for torches," Rheene offered.

"Make it quick," Owen said.

The two Wequen flew back the way they had come and returned a minute later, each with a torch clutched in their teeth. Rheene dropped his into Owen's waiting hand. Gossamer gave his to Mesna.

"Good work," said the Centaur.

Lorania reached out and touched Owen gently. "I feel stronger," she said. "She's down this tunnel. Not far. We're going to make it."

Owen smiled at the nymph. "You are brave," he said. "I am proud to know you."

Owen's tenderness hit Molly right in the bullseye of her heart. She smiled, tears in her eyes. Molly was facing the unknown, down in the dark with mythic beings, unsure if her body was still in bed after being here for *days*, hoping that Mother Nature would be able to restore order when they found her, and touched by how her new companions cared for one another. She realized how emotionally attached she'd become to them. She missed her father, but she was growing to love Rheene, Gossamer, Lorania, Owen, and Mesna as if they were family.

There was no time to express it fully.

Owen led the way down the new tunnel. It wasn't just dirt. Roots and chunks of rock poked out from the tunnel walls and ceiling, as if this new passageway was still under construction. It turned slightly a few times, but they only walked a few minutes until they reached a small door just over eight feet tall – too small for an average-sized dragon to easily enter. It was set in an arch of stones that looked like a recent installation. The door was metal, plain and dull. There was no door handle and Mesna leaned against it. It opened easily, without much sound.

"I'll go first," she said quietly to Owen.

Molly could see the Giant's dark blue eyes. They were clear and focused. Mesna turned back to the door, torch in hand, and she ducked her head as she went through.

Molly shifted to her left, trying to get a glimpse of the space through the doorway, Owen standing ready on her right. He held the door open as the Giant stood holding up her torch, illuminating the area in front her.

There was a massive room beyond the door. Half a dozen torches were along the walls, giving off enough light for Molly to be able to see four Neuos huddled around something in the middle of the room. Behind them and to the right, in the far corner of the large room, a woman was chained to the wall. Her arms were outstretched and her head hung forward, her long hair covering the front of her. Molly guessed the imprisoned woman was just over one hundred meters from the door, about the distance of one straightaway on a track field.

At first, the Neuos didn't look up: as if they had been expecting the door to be opened, but not by 'Molly's Posse.' Owen was bursting through the door by the time the first Neuo turned away from what was occupying its attention. As the Neuo stood, Molly could see what the Neuos had been focusing on: a dull sphere with a crack in it.

The Neuo who noticed Owen first cried out in a terrible screech and the others beside it turned to face the doorway.

Lorania was staring with wide eyes at the chained woman on the other side of the small group of Neuos.

"Mother Nature!" the nymph called out desperately as the Centaur rushed at the Neuos.

They had found her! Molly wanted to sprint over to the Keeper chained in the far corner of the room, but with four Neuos between Molly and Mother Nature, she didn't think she could even get close to Mother Nature before one of the Neuos would get to her.

The two small horses whinnied and followed close behind Owen.

Mother Nature raised her head. Her dark brown hair parted, revealing a beautiful face with strong features. For a moment, time stood still and Molly had a passing thought that Mother Nature looked a bit like Doris Day from the old movies she'd watched with her parents. Even in her captivity, Mother Nature's quiet dignity and raw power shone from within – an energetic intensity, weakened for the moment, but still extremely powerful. It was like the sensation Molly felt when she closed her eyes in the summer sun – a warmth she could feel over her entire body.

Suddenly, a heavy, low rumbling sound came from *behind* Molly, in the tunnel they had just come down.

Chaos! Molly thought in terror as she slipped the crystal sphere back in its sack.

But it wasn't Chaos. It sounded more like the sound of pounding feet – a stampede rushing down the tunnel toward them.

Mesna thrust her torch into the dirt and moved to intercept the Neuos with Owen. The Giant narrowed her eyes as she swung a huge fist down on the closest Neuo's head, breaking its spine and cracking its skull.

Owen reared up and kicked another Neuo so hard that Molly could hear several snapping bones. She winced at the horrific sound. The Centaur swung down with a fist and smashed another Neuo.

Mesna was already crouching down, bracing her hands on the dirt floor as she launched her right foot at the last Neuo. She kicked it hard, slamming it against the wall. Owen came down on its head with his front hooves to make sure it was down for good. The Centaur and Giant had been brutal and efficient.

The pounding sounds of running feet were joined by screams and shrieks from behind Molly. *More Neuos!* She thought wildly. *Thousands of them!* She turned to look and could see them running down the tunnel – headed right for her! In seconds, the Neuos would be at the doorway. Molly grabbed Lorania's arm and yanked the nymph through the doorway into Mother Nature's dungeon. Molly pointed at the large metal door and gave Lorania a desperate look. The nymph nodded and they used all their strength to slam the heavy door behind them.

Chapter Fifteen

Molly glanced over her shoulder and wondered if she would be able to make it to Mother Nature before the stampeding Neuos could push the door open and get to her first. She didn't think she could make it, and it would mean leaving Lorania to hold the door all by herself. Both Molly and Lorania pushed up against it with their backs with all their strength, feet digging into the ground to brace them. A second later, the Neuos slammed against the other side of the metal door. The wave of Neuos hit the door with a tremendous force and the two young women were thrown forward as the Neuos flung the door open and began to rush into the room.

Realizing their desperate situation, Owen turned to attack the Neuos rushing through the door. Rheene and Gossamer were flying on either side of his head, terrified, but ready to attack with their small hooves.

Mesna was not far behind them, jumping over Molly and Lorania, who were scrambling to get up, and slamming her shoulder against the door. Had it been made of wood, it would surely have shattered, but with the solid stone archway, and the door being made of a strong metal, it shut cleanly, crushing two Neuos as they were caught trying to squeeze through.

Unfortunately, seven Neuos had already made it through by the time the Giant had slammed the door shut.

The first Neuo that had come through raised its claws to strike Owen. Gossamer flew down and kicked its upraised arm. The Neuo let out a frustrated cry as Gossamer flew up and away from its second swipe. It was enough for Owen to swing his left arm down and grasp the Neuo's head without being prone to its claws. He twisted, snapping the Neuo's neck, and let the dead creature drop as he faced the next Neuo.

Molly was struggling to get up on her side, pulling the sack with the crystal sphere up on her shoulder. Lorania was also trying to get to her feet, looking longingly at Mother Nature.

Owen had killed another Neuo, but he was off balance as another came at him from the side. The Centaur cried out in pain as the Neuo's claws sliced deep into his side. Owen staggered, clutching at his wound.

Rheene dropped down on the Neuo that had just wounded Owen and angrily lashed out with his hooves, connecting with the Neuo's head. It slumped to the ground, bleeding profusely.

Mesna, still with her back to the door, kicked at two of the Neuos close to her, causing one to crash into the other, and both slamming against the wall, dead on impact.

By this time, Molly was back on her feet and pushing up against the door with the Giant. Lorania was up a second later, beside them.

Molly was looking at Mother Nature, wondering if she could reach the Keeper before the last two Neuos got her, or before the ones on the other side of the door pushed the door open again.

"Get the sphere to Mother Nature!" Owen shouted to Molly.

Neuo claws were beginning to tear through the metal door, inflicting shallow wounds on the Giant. Lorania was doing her best to help, desperate and frightened, as the door was slowly being shredded from the other side. Rheene and Gossamer were fending off the two Neuos that were trying to get at Owen, dropping down just above the range of their lethal claws before flying up a few feet again.

It's now or never, Molly thought desperately. *Run for it!*

Molly pulled the crystal sphere from her sack. It was no longer milky, but glowing like a neon light. At the same moment, the shredded metal door was forced open and Neuos flooded into the chamber.

Mother Nature watched hopefully as Molly, cradling the sphere like a football, used her speed to cross the room. "I need to be in contact with it!" the Keeper said weakly, but with command. "Touch me with it!"

Molly could hear the sounds of the Neuos' claws and cries behind her. They had all seen the glowing sphere and ignored her companions as they rushed to intercept her.

Molly held her breath and ran. She moved the glowing sphere in front of her belly, gripping it with both hands. She was just a few yards from Mother Nature. Molly slowed, not daring to look behind her. She stopped in front of the Keeper, reaching out with the glowing sphere desperately, almost dropping it.

The crystal sphere made contact with Mother Nature's jaw and neck.

Instantly, thick, dark green vines shot out from the walls in the dark dungeon. They moved to block the Neuos from Mother Nature, Molly, and her companions. Some of the Neuos were caught in the stream of

205

vines and were crushed and gored.

More vines shot up through the ground, and more down from the ceiling, weaving together to form thick walls. A few wove into the manacles holding Mother Nature prisoner. The vines expanded and broke the manacles apart, the pieces falling into the dirt.

Wild screams of rage and bloodlust erupted from the Neuos. They were slashing at the vines, and working their way through.

Mother Nature reached out and took the sphere from Molly. But as she did, a few of the Neuos broke free from the vine walls. With her back to them, Molly was exposed, vulnerable. The first Neuo through the wall slashed at her, driving its razor sharp claws through the soft meat of her back. She screamed in pain, twisting sideways, and fell to the dirt floor. She could only watch as the next few moments unfolded.

Mother Nature was holding the sphere with one hand, slightly behind her and her other hand reached out at the Neuos just feet away from her. Vines came up from beside Molly and lifted the Neuos up, smashing them against the ceiling. The Keeper looked furious, although her face was beautiful and her strength was growing by the second.

It burns so bad! Molly thought. The cuts didn't just hurt, they stung fiercely: as if her back had been stung by a thousand wasps. *Am I dying? Will I wake up in bed with my back cut to shreds?* She tried to move, but her arms and legs stayed where they were. She was in pain, and it was difficult to accept that she was seriously wounded. She hoped that if she died, that Mother Nature could save her new friends, and maybe even stop the Neuos from doing any more damage. She managed to raise her head a little, turning it sideways to face the action in the room. A black shape popped into view. A figure. Robed, and carrying a weapon of some kind. It was a staff with a long curved blade at the end. The Keeper, Death, was materializing in front of her.

She blinked. "I don't want to die," she whispered.

The black face beneath the hood turned towards her. "I will not take you yet," the Keeper assured her.

Behind him, Molly could see that another being had materialized as well. Medusa, the Dream Keeper. The ten yards between Molly and her companions seemed like miles. Her vision was blurred, but she could make out what was happening. Medusa was waving her arms in wide, smooth gestures. As she did, the Neuos in front of her disappeared one at a time.

Mother Nature still looked furious and was brutally crushing Neuos with the vines she was controlling. Mesna had picked Lorania up and carried the nymph over to Owen. Lorania was gently caressing the Centaur and Mesna was standing guard – even though Mother Nature and Medusa seemed to be doing just fine at taking out Neuos.

Medusa had helped clear out the makeshift dungeon. Mother Nature made a fist and violently jerked it down to her side. All of the vines pulled back into the walls and floor. The chunks of stone that had been broken when the vines had burst through, lay about the room.

Now, Mother Nature and Medusa moved to the shredded metal door and started making their way back up the tunnel. Neuos were fleeing, but the two Keepers were not content to let them escape.

The room grew lighter.

Is this that light people see when they die? Molly thought in a detached way. *Maybe I'll see Dad on the other side...if there is one. At least my friends are safe...*

A face came into view. A young face. A girl's face. It was sideways at first, but it turned and the girl's eyes were looking at Molly with relief and pride. They were odd eyes, white with huge black pupils. They did not look human.

"You found her," the face was saying.

Molly thought the face was familiar. The eyes were familiar, too, though she couldn't make a connection to anyone she knew. Things were still fuzzy and she found it difficult to stay focused.

"I may not be Mother Nature, but this is still *my* creation, and I do not like it when things suffer and die like this," the young girl continued. Her face turned sideways again. "Not at all."

Molly blinked and tried to speak. She found it difficult to breathe. Then, she saw the red mittens the girl wore. The same girl she'd seen in Littletown, the same one from her dreams, and the same one who had been with Father Time when she had started her journey to find Mother Nature.

Owen was standing behind the girl with the red mittens. He didn't look injured. Molly smiled – he was OK.

The young girl crouched down and pulled off one of her red mittens. Gently, she reached out with her bare hand and touched Molly's forehead. Instantly, Molly could breathe easily. The painful burning sensation in her back vanished. Her mind cleared. She got to her feet.

"You have helped save the Worlds and Realms!" the girl with the red mittens said to her.

Death was standing a little behind her. "You have done us all a great service – all of us," he added.

Now that her thoughts were clearer and she was putting things together, she realized just who it was standing in front of her. "*Your* creation..." Molly said. She noticed the way that Owen, Mesna, Lorania, Rheene and Gossamer were looking at the young girl. Death may have had a similar look, but his face was still hidden inside the blackness of his hood. "You're...the Creator?"

The girl stood, looking up at Molly with a big smile. The girl...the Creator...was not wearing her winter hat and the eyes that looked at Molly were almost frightening now that she knew who this being was.

"You're...like God?" Molly asked. "*The* God?"

The Creator shook her small head. "There are no gods. Only Creators and their creations."

"So, like, you're the one who really got me started on this journey," Molly said, not sure of how to act around the super powered being that wasn't a god, but still was the Creator – of a billion Worlds and a billion Realms, and trillions of living things, and rocks, and space, and dreams... "Father Time is...what? Your assistant?"

"All the Keepers are my assistants," the young girl...Creator replied. "He's more of a...consultant. When it comes to matters of cause and effect, he has very unique insight."

"And you're a little girl," Molly stated.

"Nope," the Creator replied. "I am an energy being, beyond the limits of what living things are – I can take any form I want. When I visit Earth, taking human form seems the easiest. Not a lot of imagination there yet.

Your World is a little slow at adapting to new things. If it makes any difference, there are some Worlds and Realms that are even *less* imaginative, *less* developed. But I'm a Creator. I make things to the best to my ability. The rest…just kind of happens."

"But millions of those Neuos killed…so many," said Molly, feeling like the girl didn't realize that letting things play out meant that millions of beings had just been slaughtered by the Creator's own creations.

The girl hung her head and removed her other mitten. She wiggled her fingers and played with them for a couple of seconds. "Well, I am still learning," said the Creator. There was a hint of defensiveness in the reply.

Molly wasn't sure what to say about that. "So, it's over?" she asked.

The Creator lifted her head and her smile was as big as ever. Molly had to admit that she was kind of cute and endearing, if confusing and little naïve. "The Neuos' reign of terror will come to an end, thanks to you and your companions."

Mother Nature and Medusa returned.

"They are gone," Mother Nature reported to the Creator.

"Brilliant," the Creator said, still looking at Molly. "Now, time to make things right. Shall I?"

Molly shrugged. "I guess so," she said. Molly had first thought of the girl, the Creator, as an innocent child. Now, she came off as more of an arrogant brat who was making things up as she went along. Still, Molly had done what she had set out to do. Her companions had survived, too, which she found the most rewarding aspect of her quest. Mother Nature, who still looked like a long, dark haired, and pissed off, version of Doris

Day, had been set free and given her new crystal sphere. Medusa and Death seemed to be alright as well. Death looked stronger, standing taller, and not flickering any longer. The Worlds and Realms had been saved, and now she would get to be with her father again.

But her time in the Worlds and Realms wasn't over yet.

Chapter Sixteen

The Creator raised her hand. Molly still wasn't sure if the Creator was a '*her,*' or an '*it.*' Did energy beings have genders? As the young girl's hand moved in a slow arc above her head, all the torches that were out relit. Mother Nature's crystal sphere was not glowing, but there was a soft light emanating from the area around the Creator and Keepers. All the dead Neuos were gone, along with their stench – for which Molly was very grateful. It had been days since she'd smelled anything pleasant, and the dirt around her smelled wonderful at the moment.

Mother Nature walked over to Molly. The Keeper looked Molly in the eye. No one spoke. Mother Nature held up her new crystal sphere. "They knew I would be weakened," she said. "It was a trap. To what end they wished to meet, I am not certain." She paused for a moment. "They killed, just to keep me here, forced me to use all of my will to keep Chaos from completely destroying…everything. You are deserving of the watch and the power. You are truly a Dream Walker."

"Thank you," Molly said, fingering the golden pocket watch. *Dream Walker*. She wasn't sure what it meant and was about to ask about it when the Creator spoke.

"You can explain at the Dance of the Six Moons," the Creator said to Mother Nature. "First, you and your fellow Keepers will lead us out of this pit. I wish to see what damage was done, and fix what I can."

"My sisters!" Lorania cried out.

Molly gave the nymph a sympathetic look.

The Creator turned to face Lorania and said, "I will do what I can."

Medusa, Mother Nature, and Death began to walk out of the room and into the tunnel leading up to the Tower of Raflure.

Molly went over to Owen and looked up at the magnificent Centaur. He was completely healed, standing boldly between Lorania and Mesna. Rheene and Gossamer were standing at Mesna's feet looking relieved, their alert, pointed ears not even reaching the top of the Giant's scuffed boots.

"How did all this happen?" Molly asked the Centaur. "Did the Creator heal you?"

Owen nodded, looking a little ashamed. "The instant Mother Nature touched the crystal sphere, Medusa, the Creator, and Death must have felt the power. It sent out a beacon. I bet Rheene and Gossamer can teleport now."

The two little flying horses nodded.

"It tingles," Gossamer said. "It's fading, though."

"Feels good to be myself again," Rheene added.

The others had gone through the shredded metal door and Owen started after them. Lorania jumped up on the Centaur's back and Molly walked beside Mesna as they made their way into the tunnel. Rheene and Gossamer flew, bringing up the rear.

"So, everything is going to be alright?" Molly asked Owen.

"Seems so," he replied without conviction.

They were quiet until they reached the room where the dead dragons lay among the Neuos that Owen and Mesna had killed.

"Nasty things, those Neuos," the Creator said in mild annoyance. "This needs fixing." The form of the young girl moved to the closest dead dragon and reached out to touch it: like she had done for Molly just moments ago. However, Molly had not been dead and wasn't sure what to expect. The dragon's wounds healed in seconds and the great beast shuddered for a moment as it drew in a large breath.

Medusa was up front and she flicked her wrist a few times. The dead Neuos vanished. Molly wondered where they went, but decided not to ask. She was watching the dragon as it stretched and got to its feet. It was sleek and muscular with long arms and a long snout. Its thick legs were sturdy and the reptilian being looked down at the Creator with intelligent, snake-like eyes. The living dragon's tail brushed against a dead dragon beside it and the same thing happened to the dead beast. Its wounds healed. The dragon shuddered as it took a deep breath and got to its feet. As each dragon was touched, either by the Creator or a dragon that had been brought back to life, they healed as they returned to life. In less than a minute, the room was filled with living dragons.

Molly looked at the expressions on Mother Nature and Medusa's faces. They looked impressed and a little concerned, as if they were wondering the same thing Molly was – had the Creator planned to just bring every dead being but the Neuos back to life from the beginning? To Molly, who knew very little about Creators, it seemed like the Creator was what she (it) appeared to be – a little girl, out of her league, expecting Keepers and Centaurs to do the dirty work, and coming in to clean up at the end.

Molly wasn't upset. She was curious. It seemed pretty clear that the girl Creator was not interested in what anyone else thought, only concerned with doing what she wanted to at the moment.

"Keep moving!" the Creator urged, waving a hand in a shooing gesture at the three Keepers a few yards in front of her.

"Look at that!" Gossamer said in awe, looking at the dragons. "As if they'd never died."

Mother Nature and Medusa began to move forward again, but Death remained for a moment. His posture was odd, as if he was offended, but also thankful. Molly wondered if it was just his posture, or if it was some kind of magical way that Death had of expressing himself – without facial expressions.

"Where did the Neuos go?" one of the dragons asked. "They were just here! Attacking us!"

"All gone!" the Creator said. "And I brought you back to life!"

The dragons looked uncertain, each doing their best to come to terms with having been killed by Neuos and then being brought back from the dead.

The Creator noticed that Death had not moved from his spot yet, still holding his scythe, head tilted slightly down under his hood, giving the impression that he was deep in thought.

"Don't look so down!" the young girl Creator said to him. "You are still needed. Now get up there with your sisters!"

Death nodded and moved quickly, almost gliding, to catch up to the Dream Keeper and Mother Nature.

The Creator got to the other side of the room and spoke in a voice so loud that it rose above the murmuring voices of the recently resurrected dragons. "Rebuild Raflure!" she said, and then exited the large room a few steps behind the Keepers.

They went through the next tunnel to the staircase with the large stairs. Lorania got down off of Owen's back, ready to climb the stairs. But before they could start their climb, Medusa flicked her wrist and everyone floated up a few inches off the ground. They glided up the stairs smoothly and quickly with Medusa's aid. Molly thought it was almost like riding a magical escalator. When they got to the top, the Dream Keeper flicked her wrist again and they all gently lowered back to the ground.

The Keepers continued to lead the way out. Molly followed behind the Creator, holding Lorania's hand. The nymph seemed to be in a daze. She looked happy, relieved, and uncertain. Rheene and Gossamer flew beside her, also looking unsure about what was going to happen next. Owen and Mesna were at the back of the group. Whenever Molly glanced back at them, the Giant and Centaur were talking softly to each other. Molly couldn't tell if they were upset or excited. The Creator was ignoring them all for the most part.

They arrived at the room where they had come across the first Neuo in the Tower, the one that had killed three dragons. Again, Medusa waved her hand and the dead Neuo vanished. The Creator touched the nearest dragon, bringing it back to life. Then, instead of going over to touch the other two, the Creator impatiently waved her small hand toward them, bringing them to life.

"What happened?" one of the dragons asked as he flexed his long reptilian fingers. "Were we dead?"

"Yes," the Creator said with a bob of her head. "But, as the Creator, I feel like I need to undo the damage caused by the Neuos. Now that they're gone, it is time to rebuild."

The three dragons looked at the form of the young girl with their large golden eyes. Molly thought that while they looked snake-like, she'd seen frogs and lizards with similar eyes.

"The Creator?" one of the dragons asked.

There was a sudden, brilliant flash of light. Where the Creator's form of a young girl had been, was now a large light blue sphere of electrical energy. It sizzled and crackled as it hovered, making Molly's hair begin to rise. She noticed that it was happening to Lorania and Mother Nature as well.

"DO YOU PREFER MY TRUE FORM?" the Creator asked in a voice as powerfully intense as its electric form.

Now Molly was *sure* that the Creator was just showing off.

"If you wish," the dragon responded in a startled and defensive tone.

There was another flash of light and the Creator's form changed back into a normal-sized human child about eight years old. Now that Molly was paying attention, the Creator looked a little bit older than she had the last time they were together.

"Let's keep going," the Creator said. "We're almost out of the Tower."

When they got to the door that opened out into the city, Medusa flicked her wrist again and the doors opened. The terrible smell of death hit and Molly covered her nose.

The Creator waved a hand and the smell vanished. Stepping out into Raflure under that orange-red sky, she spoke. Her voice did not rise in volume, yet it carried throughout the city, down every street and road.

"Rise," she said. "Healed, and ready to rebuild."

The dragons lying around them stirred. Medusa and Mother Nature looked on, their blank expressions hiding their thoughts. The dragons' wounds healed as they began to breathe. As if waking from a mass slumber, the dragons got to their feet. Death was facing the Creator. Molly felt as though she could feel his emotions. He was clearly upset, disturbed by what the Creator was doing. However, he held back whatever was on his mind. He had spoken very little since arriving.

"As I said," the Creator said to him, "this is only to set things right. All will return to normal very soon."

Molly wondered what the Creator considered 'normal.'

The dragons around them moved about. Some flapped their wings and took flight. Molly looked on in wonder as the great creatures soared. They were magnificent.

As she was looking up, Molly suddenly realized just how wonderful what the Creator was doing really was. The Creator may be acting somewhat childish, but these dragons hadn't done anything wrong as far as she knew. What was the harm in bringing life back to them after what the Neuos had done? Molly realized that she might have done the same thing in the Creator's place. Wasn't she here because she'd wanted her father back from the dead?

The feeling of relief was contagious. Now, Lorania was grinning, hopping up and down on her bare feet. Rheene and Gossamer were lightly flapping their wings as they stood beside Molly, also looking up at the airborne dragons. Mesna had a thoughtful smile, while Owen stood perfectly still with his arms crossed over his chest not looking as impressed as the others. His tail was swishing in a twitchy way. Molly saw him lock eyes with Medusa and the look they gave one another was both one of understanding, and one like parents putting up with a child's playful antics.

The form of the young girl stretched out her arms, a wave of warm light radiated from them. The orange-red sky turned a beautiful shade of soft violet as the warmth emanating from the Creator passed over and through Molly like a waterless shower. After it passed, she felt refreshed, clean. Her clothes were spotless. The canteen and pouch with the food were gone. All the dirt and grime from their journey had washed away.

"Much better," the Creator said, sounding quite pleased. "It will spread…to other Realms…other Worlds." The girl closed her eyes, smiling, breathed in once slowly, and opened her eyes as she breathed out. "Clean," the Creator said.

Molly wondered how the Creator even needed to breathe. Perhaps it was like those stories from myths where gods liked to visit Earth in human form to experience human life. Now that she was thinking about it, many of those mythical gods did some rather despicable things. Could some of those stories actually be true? That thought reminded her of what the Creator had said; that there were no gods – only Creator's and

219

their creations. Once again, answers only led to more questions.

"I can take it from here," the Creator said to the Keepers. "Prepare for the ceremony. I will see you at the Dance of the Six Moons."

Without a word, the three Keepers vanished.

"Now," the Creator said, turning to look at the nymph. "Let's go see about your sisters!"

One moment they were all standing outside the Tower of Raflure. The next they were by a lake and wooded area.

"Home!" Lorania shouted. "Oh, thank you!" the nymph said earnestly as she let go of Molly's hand. She peered into the woods hopefully.

"Just in time for the celebration at the Dance of the Six Moons!" the Creator said. "You will all be recognized for what you have done to help save my creation from Chaos."

Two nymphs burst out from the woods, arms outstretched as they ran toward Lorania.

"Sasha! Naomi!" Lorania cried out happily as tears of joy filled her large eyes.

"Tonight," the Creator said looking at Molly, "you stay with the nymphs. Tomorrow, we hold the ceremony and join the Dance." Her face grew more serious, but she was still smiling. "Then, you will return to Littletown."

Chapter Seventeen

It was a beautiful evening. The wind was light and warm. The air smelled of flowers. Molly was propped up with her back against a large tree. Rheene was sitting on her right, nestled up to her thigh. His small head was resting just above her knee. Gossamer was on her left, head in her lap, her left hand cradling him. Mesna was stretched out in the grass a few feet from them, eyes closed in the evening sunlight.

Owen was off somewhere. He hadn't explained much. After the Creator vanished, the Centaur had stated that he was going to meet up with Medusa and that he'd be back before the Dance of the Six Moons began.

Lorania was with her sisters, playing among the trees. They laughed, sang, danced, and hugged each other. It was like watching happy children on a playground.

Molly hadn't been this relaxed the entire time she'd been in the Worlds and Realms. Only, she hadn't actually been to a World other than Earth yet. Still, with Chaos out of the way, and the Creator off to do what she could about the devastation caused by the Neuos, Molly felt like they deserved a little reprieve. She was still excited at the prospect of seeing her father again, yet she was glad that she had some time with her new friends before she went back to her mundane life in Littletown.

"Seems like Raflure was a long time ago," Molly said sleepily. "Almost surreal."

"What does that mean?" Gossamer asked. "Surreal?"

"Like things are not really...*real*," Molly replied, petting the small light brown flying horse. It was like having a large cat or medium-sized dog on her lap. She found it comforting. However, having a conversation with him was something she'd never done with any of the animals she'd had on her lap before. "With everything we saw, it can be hard to believe that it was real."

"I was there," said Gossamer flatly. "It was real."

Molly let out a snort. "Yeah, but it feels like it happened months ago, or to someone else. That's what I meant by it being surreal."

Gossamer shook his mane a little and flicked his ears. "Sounds like nonsense to me," he said. "Either something is real, or it isn't. Right, Rheene?"

Rheene lifted his head. "I guess so," he replied. "I'm not much of a deep thinker. Maybe everything is real. Maybe not."

Molly laughed. "Well, you guys may be professionals, but you're certainly not philosophers."

Mesna smiled and looked up at Molly. The Giant looked as though she was thinking hard about something. Her face was serious, even though her smile was genuine. Mesna's dark blue eyes looked far away. She sat up. Molly looked up at the Giant as she spoke. "We have enough philosophers," Mesna said. "Its friends, allies, and kindness we need more of. Like what we have here, right now, in this moment."

Even though it sounded a little sappy to Molly, she knew that it was true. Car accidents caused by drunken drivers that tore families apart, beings that could wipe out cities larger than any on Earth – the things that hurt people and made life harder than it needed to be – she didn't want any of that. She wanted evenings like this, hanging out with friends. She wanted to spend time playing cards with her parents and laughing with her friends. Molly enjoyed running, creating, and exploring, but after going through her recent ordeal, she just wanted to relax with her new friends for a while. She didn't want to rush back to Littletown. She was going to cherish the time she had with them.

"Crazy to think that my body could still be sleeping in bed back home," Molly said as her mind wandered. "Time and space…" She paused and tapped her index finger on Gossamer's nose. "It's surreal."

Gossamer looked up at her with a blank stare, flicked his ears, and then looked back at the nymphs.

"Astral projection," said the Giant in a thoughtful tone, "Traveling beyond the body, while still maintaining control of the mind through sheer will. I have seen it before, but never like I have with you, Molly. Not just fascinating, but something special. You're making me more interested in you and your story than the history of the major cities in the Worlds and Realms."

Molly tilted her head as she pet both Rheene and Gossamer. They seemed as content as possible. She was glad that just touching them didn't teleport her. "I always wanted to believe that things like going to other Worlds was possible. Earth seems kinda boring now." She thought about her town, her family and friends, sports, music and art. Brian Carter. It wasn't all boring, although she wondered what she'd do when she went back. Would it all seem like a dream? Could she go back and be her old self?

"What's Earth like?" Mesna asked Molly, turning her thoughtful eyes on her.

Molly shrugged. "It's alright. We've got forests, oceans, deserts, storms, and all sorts of plants and animals. The animals don't talk like you guys," she said to Rheene and Gossamer. "But there's also crummy things, too…like school, bullies, chores, wars, and politics."

Mesna laughed. It was so sudden and bold that it startled Rheene and Gossamer. Molly felt them stiffen up for a second. For the first time, other than her sheer size, or how she pounded Neuos, she sounded exactly like how a Giant should sound. Like cats, Rheene and Gossamer relaxed and pretended as though nothing had happened. They were cool customers. Molly smiled. She still thought that they were the most adorable living things ever.

"Those things are everywhere," the Giant said. "Especially politics and war. Still, maybe I will visit Earth someday."

Molly grinned. "That would be so cool! I can't imagine how awesome it would be to have you guys to hang out with me back home. What would people say if they saw you? It would probably freak them out…That would be so awesome!"

"It will have to wait. I think after the Dance of the Six Moons we'll all be quite busy," the Giant said thoughtfully. "How those Neuos could Travel to other Worlds and Realms isn't just a mystery, it's a serious concern – especially if millions of them remain unaccounted for. I expect Mother Nature and the Gate Keeper are trying to figure that out – if they haven't already."

"Too bad Owen couldn't be here with us," Molly said.

"He's as amazing as the legends say," Rheene said with pride. "He's the standard for being a professional! You know, it wasn't long after the Chaln invasion that we were created," he said, sounding very much like a scholar. "The Centaurs defeated them, freed all the prisoners of war, and Owen led the charge. I can imagine how amazing that must have been," said Rheene in admiration. "Never mind the Neuo that got him," he added. "We were all in bad shape, and outnumbered. He was still amazing – and would have died for us."

"Owen scared me the first time I saw him," Molly admitted, smiling to herself. "He's tough, and looks it. Not just because he can toss trees around and kill Neuos, though. He's mentally tough. But under all of that toughness is a kind and gentle guy."

There was a moment where the four of them were silent as they thought about the journey they had undergone with the Centaur. They watched the nymphs play a game like hide and seek; where the nymphs would actually blend in to the trees and then giggle when they found each other. There about twenty nymphs enjoying the evening's game.

Lorania was staying close to Naomi and Sasha, holding their hands and hugging them as often as possible.

"I love watching them," Molly said. "So much fun in how they play. No one is cheating or calling names."

"Hey, hey," Gossamer said. "Calling names *is* fun!"

"That's what you think..." Molly said playfully, "...big butt."

Gossamer's head whipped round, his eyes wide. "Big, eh?" His left wing pointed up at her face. "At least I don't have windows on my face...window face."

Molly giggled and straightened her glasses. They'd been back on since the Creator had left them here with the nymphs. "Pot belly," she shot back.

Rheene made a whinnying sound and flapped his wings a little. "He's a pot belly alright."

Gossamer turned to his companion. "Yeah, well, I didn't name myself after *food*, manure machine."

Molly laughed. It felt good to be silly with her friends. Even Mesna was smiling, although she didn't join in.

They called each other some more silly names and then talked about random things. They were invited to share a meal with the nymphs that consisted of fruits and nuts, and a drink that was like coconut water. It was a happy evening and when they settled down for the night, Molly was asleep in seconds.

The next morning they shared a similar meal of fruits and nuts, but with tea and cinnamon oats. (Rheene and Gossamer had two helpings of the oats.)

Lorania had talked a little about the Dance of the Six Moons the night before. It was an old tradition, a celebration of life that was recognized by most of the Realms and many Worlds. From what the nymph said, it seemed to Molly that it was basically the first holiday – ever. The Creator had brought forth existence and in the Realm of Timeless Wisdom they stopped to take part in festivities to commemorate that life had begun here. When all six moons were aligned in the sky, beings gathered to dance, sing, eat, and drink. Lorania had made it sound like a pretty good time and Molly was looking forward to it.

As they were finishing breakfast, the first beings began to show up. They were the small bear-like creatures Molly had seen in the stone city when Chaos had struck, and she'd seen a few dead ones in Raflure. They had long snouts like bears but their paws were more like furry human hands. They walked upright and also had feet instead of paws. Not one of them was walking on all fours. Their bushy little tails were cute and they looked like simple, carefree creatures – similar to how the nymphs were. Molly was not surprised that they were the first to arrive. They were called Fo-Pas. Molly knew a little French and was aware that 'faux pas' was a term for an embarrassing mistake. However, the little dancing bears didn't seem like mistakes at all.

"We heard there was to be some dancing and singing tonight!" one of them said energetically as they mingled with the nymphs. He scratched one of his short ears and added, "I hope you don't mind if I start a little early!"

Sasha, Lorania's sister, dashed over to him, took his paw hands in hers and said, "Not at all! Let's dance!"

She whirled him around and they spun out of sight amongst the trees.

One of the other Fo-Pas came up to Molly and was looking at the pocket watch around her neck. "A human," the small bear-like being said in a heavy female voice. "With a Keeper's watch! Is the danger over?" she asked, sounding concerned.

"As far as I know," Molly said. She lifted the golden watch up and then dropped it. "This is what I need to Travel. Nothing to be afraid of."

"Oh, I see," the Fo-Pa said, sounding relived. "We can dance without worry. The *only* way to dance!"

By midday, dragons, Centaurs (Owen was with them), the dark-skinned people with angel wings she'd seen at the gates of Raflure, fairies, unicorns, Giants, ugly bug-like creatures called Ha-Nee-Nee that had four black eyes and a dozen thin legs, the Siren, the Cyclops, and many more beings familiar and unfamiliar to Molly had arrived. She had stopped asking Mesna which ones were called what after a short while because there were too many to remember.

The Cyclops, with the Siren at his side, found Molly. He looked relived. "I could not see if you survived the attack," he said. "Clearly, my vision was not complete."

"Thanks for keeping it to yourself," Molly replied in an attempt to be nonchalant. It came out a little sarcastic, but the Cyclops didn't seem to notice. "Just glad I could do it, and get a chance to save my dad."

"A deserving reward," he said, and then departed with the Siren, who gave Molly a nod and beautiful smile, as they made their way over to Owen and the Centaurs.

A few minutes later, one of the winged men with dark skin came over to Molly and bowed. "I am grateful for what you've done," he said. "I am alive because of you. You will be remembered by my people for as long as history is told."

Molly blushed, feeling a little embarrassed, but also touched and proud. "Thanks," she said. She pointed at Rheene, Gossamer, and Mesna (who had been by her side the entire time) and said, "I couldn't have done it without them." She reached back and touched the spot where the flying bit of stone had cut her elbow. It was a small scar, healed just like the wounds in her back when the Creator had touched her. However, for some reason, there were no scars on her back.

The winged man bowed to them and said, "Many thanks."

"You're not angels, are you?" Molly asked him.

The man smiled. A few of the women and men with him laughed a little. "No," he said. "Far from it." He held out a hand as if asking for a dance. "Will you grant me the honor of a dance later this evening?" he asked, now serious again.

Molly felt her face flush a little more. He was handsome. "Ah...I guess so," she replied.

"Excellent!' he exclaimed. "My name is Narru. I look forward to that dance." He bowed again. "Until then, I bid you a good day."

He moved off with his people to mingle.

There were thousands and thousands of beings around the wooded area and lake now. It was starting to look like a massive tailgating party. Food was being prepared and cooked. There were small groups dancing. Others were talking and laughing raucously. Hugs, smiles, and joy were everywhere.

Dozens of different beings came up to thank her and her companions all day. Shortly before the Dance of the Six Moons began, Lorania found Molly and said that this was the most excitement she'd ever seen at this

229

ceremony. The nymph's eyes were bright, full of anticipation and happiness.

When the Keepers arrived, it signaled the start of the celebration.

The Dance of the Six Moons began as it always had. Mother Nature stood in the middle of the field between the lake and the forest. The nymphs, hundreds of them, formed a circle around her. There was a hush over the massive gathering – Molly guessed there were hundreds of thousands of beings, maybe even over a million because they were so spread out – waiting for the final moon to rise into place. As it rose, the nymphs began to sing. It was a slow, melancholy song.

When the disc of the sixth moon was fully visible in the sky, drums began to pound. Molly couldn't see who was playing them. She was standing a few yards from the nymphs, beside her new friends, with the thousands of other participants behind her and facing her as they formed a huge circle around Mother Nature and the nymphs.

Shortly after the drums began, the dancing commenced. The nymphs changed their song, now faster, their voices filled with joy. Other beings began to join the song.

The moons were so bright that it was almost like being outside on a very cloudy day. Each of the moons was casting a shadow and the combination of all six was a little disorienting, but also quite stunning to behold. The music swelled and the dancing continued. There was plenty of room. No one had crowded too close to anyone else and Molly found that the infectious music and energy of the Dance's participants were affecting her in a powerfully emotional way. It was not possible for her to keep her feet still.

Lorania pulled away from the nymphs to join Molly, Owen, Mesna, Rheene, and Gossamer. The two small flying horses weren't actually dancing; they flitted about above Molly and Lorania back and forth to the music.

The music was beautiful, sung by hundreds of thousands of voices. The sheer amount of positive and joyful energy around her was overwhelming. It was the exact opposite of what she'd experienced in Raflure. That was death. This was life. She was alive – more alive than at any other time in her life. Tears fell. She did not care. Others around her were crying, too – unconcerned about who saw their tears or imperfect dance steps.

There was a pattern to the dance now and Molly found it almost a natural thing to simply follow along. She danced with partner after partner: a nymph one moment, a Giant the next. It was strange to bend down to the level of a Fo-Pa, and then reach up to a Centaur. But it only felt odd for about dozen partners. She got used to it quickly, as if that was part of the dance. She was wrapped up in the moment, part of something wonderful and greater than herself.

Suddenly, Narru, the winged man, was dancing with her. He was smiling. "I have come to collect!" he said, trying to be heard over the singing voices.

Molly, caught up in the dance, just nodded, smiling, and took his hand without missing a step.

And so it went for a time. Molly did not pay attention, only went along with the throng of dancers, enjoying every step, note, partner, and smile.

When the singing and dancing stopped some time later, Molly stood in a daze. She was dizzy, breathless, tired, and very happy. The crowd was parting as Mother Nature was making her way through it, toward Molly. Following close behind the Keeper were Medusa, Father Time, the Gate Keeper, and Death.

When Mother Nature reached Molly the throng had fallen quiet. The moons were in different spots in the sky, and all eyes were on the five Keepers.

Mother Nature was wearing a white gown that fluttered in the night breeze. Its narrow shoulder straps exposed Mother Nature's strong, yet feminine shoulders. Her dark hair flowed to her waist. She looked like a goddess. Molly could feel the power radiating from the Keeper in way she hadn't experienced before. With the other Keepers behind Mother Nature, there was a new, authoritative, intense feeling of power with them all gathered together. The Keepers formed a circle around Molly, standing a few feet apart from each other.

"The Dance of the Six Moons is the oldest tradition in the Realm of Timeless Wisdom," Mother Nature said in a loud, clear voice. "A tradition carried on throughout the ages, signifying the birth of existence…a moment to share in the joy of *being*." Mother Nature raised the crystal sphere up over her head. "Had this young woman from Earth not delivered me this crystal sphere, I would not be here to take part in this tradition. Nor," she paused to look around for a couple of seconds, "many of you."

A cheer went up, a multitude of voices shouting a brief note of praise.

Mother Nature dropped the sphere to her waist and held up an empty hand. The cheer silenced.

"Chaos," Medusa said in a loud voice. "Not a legend or fairy tale. A threat, real, and more serious than any I have ever known."

Molly turned a little so that she was facing Medusa. The Dream Keeper was on Mother Nature's right, dressed in a lightweight dress, similar to the one she had been wearing when Molly had first met her in the small stone castle. It was a brilliant green, matching the Dream Keeper's emerald eyes.

Medusa bent down and put a hand on Molly's shoulder. "When it was decided that the Keepers needed help to maintain order throughout the Worlds and Realms, it was not Chaos we intended to fight. But this one here, Molly Parker, daughter of Jack, from Earth, has risen above, done the near-impossible, and has earned the right to be called a Dream Walker!"

The cheer that went up was twice as loud as the last. Molly didn't know what a Dream Walker was, but she'd heard it a few times now and it seemed like a great honor. Maybe it was like being knighted or given a ceremonial key to the city. Whatever it was, it was clear that it was something special and rare.

When the voices died down a moment later, the Gate Keeper took a step forward and Molly turned a little to face him.

"The ability to Travel, unrestricted between World and Realm, to be called upon in times of need," he said, also in a loud voice that carried across the land. He held out a hand to Molly, palm up, in a giving gesture. "A Dream Walker. Worthy of the greatest power and respect."

There was a small cheer. Molly realized that the Gate Keeper's words were more for her than anyone else – and it explained a little. She hadn't just gone on a quest to get the sphere to Mother Nature. She'd been chosen, selected to carry out a mission that made her a Dream Walker – someone who could Travel the Worlds and Realms whenever she wanted, however she wanted, and when there was trouble. She was capable of doing extraordinary things. At least, she thought that's what the Gate Keeper meant.

When Death lifted his scythe, Molly turned to him, wondering what he was about to do. She wasn't afraid of him, be she was curious if he was about to take a swipe at her and send her back into her own World. But he did not. Instead, he lowered the scythe to the grass and stood up, Father Time right beside him.

"I have seen many deaths," Death said in his soft voice. It also carried like the other Keeper's voices, as if by an unseen magic. "Some just, some unjust. I do not decide which, only take the spirit to where it next must go. Jack Parker has been taken by this scythe." Death pointed a thin finger at the weapon on the ground. "Tonight, he is released."

There was no cheer, but Molly had been waiting to hear something like it and she grinned. Her eyes blurred with tears. She'd done it. She reached out and gave Death an awkward hug. She stepped back and wiped her eyes. His robes, his figure, had not been rough or cold. He had felt comforting and warm.

Father Time was standing on Death's right, to Mother Nature's left. He was wearing a fine royal blue cloak with a thick rope-like gold belt and royal blue boots. He looked vibrant and younger, though his long beard had not changed one bit. His eyes sparked, as if with unimaginable possibilities and wonders yet to be discovered.

"The Dream Walker, Molly Parker!" he said, louder than anything the other Keepers had said.

There was another cheer. Short. It felt as though this little moment of recognition was almost over.

"Free to Travel the Worlds and Realms!" he said to her, a sparkle in his eyes. "A heroine to all, and a welcome friend to the Keepers." He looked behind Molly to where her companions stood watching. "But Molly did not do this alone! Let us recognize and give thanks to those who helped this new Dream Walker! The Wequen, Rheene and Gossamer!" There was a cheer. The two small flying horses flew up proudly to be seen. "The nymph, Lorania!" Owen helped the nymph up on his back and she stood, waving with a shy grin and happy eyes. "The Centaur, Owen!" He nodded and held up a hand. "And the Giant, Mesna!" She was already taller than the others around her, but she lifted a hand up like the Centaur had done. Molly found it humorous that she looked as shy as Lorania had – maybe even more so.

Molly looked upon her companions, her new dear friends. She remembered the way that Gossamer and Rheene had flown away in terror from Chaos, and yet how they had fought the Neuos to protect her and a wounded Owen. She recalled how Mesna had been ready to take on whatever lay ahead, storming into the underground dungeon where Mother Nature had been held captive. She remembered the way Lorania had looked after Chaos had torn apart her forest and taken the nymph's sisters. She smiled, thinking of how curious the nymph found the pocket watch and the photo on the inside of the lid. She thought it was funny that Lorania had referred to the pocket watch as a *time machine*. If Molly had been the heart of her posse, then the nymph had been the soul. The Centaur had been her champion, a powerful being that had fought and been wounded by her side. He'd shown kindness and gentleness as well – even laughing a couple of times, as he had in the cave when she had mentioned fixing the timeline.

Molly had not seen them then as she saw them now. Not just her companions, but heroes and heroines in their own right. 'Molly's Posse.' She admired them. They were her friends – in some ways even closer to her than her long-time friends back in Littletown, Candice and Cindy. She would miss them. However, since she was a Dream Walker now, she guessed that she could come back whenever she wanted to see them again. Knowing that she was heading back to Littletown was bittersweet.

She lifted the golden pocket watch that was still hanging from her neck and rubbed the engraved train on the cover. She was overcome with emotion, but glad to be a part of something great, something wonderful, and fully appreciating how much her new friends meant to her. They had gone through a city of death together, fought and nearly died together.

The Keepers moved back into a small group and Molly realized that the Dream Walker ceremony was over.

The Dance began again and Molly joined in. One by one the moons set. The nymphs went back into the forest. Large groups of beings began to leave.

As the dancing broke off, Molly found the form of the Creator standing beside her – the young girl with bangs covering most of her strange eyes, but no longer wearing the red mittens. Rheene, Gossamer, Owen, and Mesna remained. There were not many others around them. A few were lying down, a few (mostly Fo-Pas) were dancing far off, and some were just standing and talking amongst themselves. Molly hadn't seen the Keepers leave, but they were nowhere in sight.

"Time to bid them farewell," the Creator said to Molly.

Rheene trotted forward a few steps and Molly bent down to embrace him. She wrapped her arms around him and held his head against her cheek. She could feel him squirming a little.

"I couldn't have done it without you," Molly said gratefully, but also feeling sad. "Thank you for being *you*…for being my *friend*."

"Your quest was the most elaborate one that Gossamer and I have ever been part of!" the small white horse said. "You have more courage and determination than most, Molly. Thank you for being my friend – we don't get to make friends very often."

Molly let him go and he stepped back as Gossamer moved up in front of his companion. The small light brown flying horse lifted his head proudly and said, "Your professionalism is admirable. However, your friendship is invaluable."

Molly grinned, a tear falling, as she reached out to pet Gossamer lightly. "I'm going to miss you, and your humor," she said.

Gossamer spread his wings wide and bowed in an elaborate way. "You are a Dream Walker now!" he said in mocking, but playful way. "You can come and go as you like. Even to see busy little guys like us," he finished, withdrawing his wings and standing up again.

"I'd like to take you back with me," Molly said, giving the Wequen a brief hug. "But I know how professional you are and wouldn't want to deprive you of your duty."

Gossamer turned to Rheene and said, "She's good. Almost as good as we are." He looked back up at Molly and shook his mane. "You deserve to be a Dream Walker. Don't forget that."

"I won't," Molly replied.

Mesna bent down gracefully, the Giant still reminding Molly of how cat-like she was in her movements. The Giant was smiling, her intelligent eyes looking deeply into Molly's – as if trying to discover more about Molly through the gaze. "I wish I could have joined your… *Posse*…sooner than I did. Maybe next time you come, I'll be able to spend more time with you, get to know you even better."

"I'd like that," Molly said. "As I said to them," she pointed at Rheene and Gossamer, "I couldn't have done it without you. I'm going to miss you."

Mesna humbly bowed her head, smiling. "And I, you," she said. "Thank you, Molly Parker…Dream Walker."

"I still don't really know what that means," Molly said, hands on her hips.

Mesna reached down and gently took one of Molly's hands in hers. "You will. No hurry. Take care, my friend. I look forward to when next we meet."

Molly straightened her glasses with her free hand. "Me, too."

Lorania had been making her way up behind Rheene and Gossamer and they parted a little to let her through. The Giant stood and stepped back as the nymph approached Molly with great big tears in her large eyes. She was wearing a new dress, light, and almost see-through. She looked almost like the ghost of a beautiful child.

Lorania did not say anything, just threw her arms around Molly and held her as tight as she could.

Molly found herself more choked up than she'd been with Rheene, Gossamer, or Mesna. "I…I…" she stammered. "I'm…glad you're back with your sisters."

Lorania released her grip and pulled back to look at Molly. "You're my sister, too," she said. "The best kind of sister – one that loves me for who I am, not because we were born under the same canopy of trees." The nymph was weeping, but her words were clear and not hampered by sobs. "We grew together, forming something new."

Molly let her own tears fall. Her smile remained. "We…healed the land," Molly said through her tears. "Together."

The nymph nodded and backed away. She turned, not saying anything more, and headed back to the trees. Lorania turned once, waved, and then vanished among the tree trunks.

Owen thrust a hand out. "I doubt this is good-bye for us. It was an honor to be by your side. You have shown true leadership and strength. Things you will need for what will come next."

Molly wasn't sure what he meant, but didn't really care either. She was too emotional. The Centaur's parting wasn't as sad, though. Maybe it was because he was so sure that they would meet again.

"I didn't think you were a big softie when I saw you with Medusa in that small castle," Molly said. Her tears were fading. She thought it also might have something to do with how the Centaur's presence seemed to radiate a sense of control. It had been shaken in Raflure, but had come back as strong as ever when he had returned for the Dance of the Six Moons. "But your heart is as big as the rest of you," Molly finished.

Owen swished his tail once and smiled warmly. "Thank you. Not something I hear very often."

Molly shrugged. "Maybe you hang with the wrong people?"

Owen laughed. "More serious ones, for sure," he said, glancing at Rheene and Gossamer before looking back at Molly. "Seriously," he said jovially, "I consider it a great honor to know you, and see you earn your place as a Dream Walker."

The Creator held up a hand to Molly. "Time to return," said the voice of the young girl.

Molly took one good, last look at her friends. They were looking back at her in a way that made her not want to go. But she knew that she must, and that she would see them again…eventually.

Molly breathed in, wiped her tears, straightened her glasses again, and touched the Creator's small hand.

Molly and the Creator were standing in the middle of Main Street in Littletown. Snow was falling lightly around them. It was quiet, no one else was around, and it was night. The streetlights were the only source of light. All the buildings on Main Street were dark inside, their storefronts lit by the streetlights. Molly and the Creator were out in front of the library.

The snow began to fall heavier, the flakes blocking more of the light. Molly could barely see the buildings on either side of her.

"Is this the dream?" she asked the Creator. "Or am I home?"

"The dream," the Creator replied. "Come."

The form of the young girl that the Creator had chosen led Molly away from the direction of her apartment. In a few seconds, Molly could see something in the middle of the street a few paces away.

After a few more steps, she made out the small grass mound that was covered by the invisible half-bubble, like a reverse snow-globe.

"This is where your father was," the Creator said. "Waiting, unaware of time."

"After he…" Molly had meant to say 'died' but she did not speak the word.

"Perhaps," the Creator said. "The explanation is not worthy to give. But this is where you began, the same point at which I met you. When you wake, Father Time's spell will cast you – and you alone – back to the morning of the accident, as promised."

They stepped inside the bubble, onto the grass mound. They sat down, facing each other.

"Will it all just…be like a dream?" Molly asked. "Will I remember everything?"

The Creator let go of Molly's hand. "You will remember everything. And only you will remember the last year of your life here. It isn't your father's timeline you changed, but your own."

"So, keep the time-travel to myself or people will think I've gone crazy," Molly said, nodding. "Gotcha."

"You will live the last year of your life over," the Creator said. "It's the only way. Your spirit and mind can travel back in time – not your body."

"Got it," Molly said, thinking about retaking her driver's test and the other annoyances she hadn't fully considered before. But the more she thought about it, the less concerned she was. She was going to have that whole year with her father! That would make it different, as if retaking tests and talking about the same movies were small things in comparison. "I guess that's cool, since Dad will be there with me."

"I like Littletown," the Creator said, changing the subject. "There are some interesting people here. Some very *gifted* people, other than you."

"What do you mean?" Molly asked, a little intrigued. Could there be other Dream Walkers here? Or, better yet, could there be Wequen, like Rheene or Gossamer, coming and going through Littletown all the time?

"Let's just put it like this," the Creator said, sounding playful again, and very much like a child, "keep an eye out for people with *special* abilities. Some are here, some have yet to arrive. You'll know who, and when." The Creator looked up at Molly. Once more, Molly thought the form of the young girl looked as though it may be a year older than the one she'd first met. "Remember all that has happened."

Molly recalled the hand sticking out from the rubble when Chaos had struck the stone city, the stench of the Neuos, and the countless dead in the streets of Raflure. There were some things she would remember without the fondness that she had for Rheene, Gossamer, Lorania, Owen, and Mesna.

"It will be tough to forget," Molly said. She reached back, outside the invisible dome, and put her hand in the snow. She pulled in a handful.

"What are you doing with that?" the Creator asked.

"Making a snowball," Molly replied casually. "Because I'm going to throw it at you."

"Why?" the Creator asked.

"Because I wanna," Molly said, still casual. "And because you deserve it!" she hurled the snowball directly at the Creator, who sat just a few feet away.

The Creator lifted her small hand and batted the ball away, breaking it apart, laughing. The Creator jumped up, ran out into the heavily falling snow, and began making a snowball of her own.

Molly got up and followed, bending down to scoop up snow as she went after the Creator. But the Creator had already made a nice, solid snowball and hit Molly with it directly on the hip.

"Oh!" Molly said, smiling. "You're going to get it!" She launched her snowball and the Creator covered her head with her arms, giggling like the child she appeared to be.

They laughed, falling into the snow. They looked at each other as the snow fell in the darkness around them.

The Creator giggled again and then started kicking out her legs and arms, waving them back and forth. It took Molly a couple of seconds to realize that the Creator was making a snow angel. Molly could feel the cold starting to creep in through her clothes, but she didn't care. She kicked out her arms and legs, making her own snow angel.

They stood up to admire their work.

It was still. The only sounds were their breathing and the soft, light tinkling sound of the falling snow.

"It's time," the Creator said. "I must go, and you must wake."

Molly was smiling, unsure of what to say.

"Stop the accident," the Creator said. "Save your father."

Molly shrugged. "That's the plan," she replied.

The form of the young girl faded and then was gone, leaving Molly alone. The grass mound and bubble over it faded at the same time. The snow swirled. Molly fell back, as if pushed by a blast of wind. She was falling backward...

Chapter Eighteen

Molly's eyes snapped open as she gasped for breath. She wasn't falling, but lying down, at home, in her bed. The golden pocket watch on the golden chain was still around her neck. She sat up.

"I remember everything," she whispered to herself, a satisfied grin on her face. "Rheene, Gossamer, Owen, the Keepers, Neuos…Raflure, and the Dance of the Six Moons." She felt it, too. Long distance running was something she did often, but not journeys that took days. She was tired and her body was a little sore, as one would expect after long, strenuous exercise.

She looked over at the window facing town. No snow. Not a single flake. There were Halloween decorations all around, but no snowstorm.

Molly shot a glance at the painting of Littletown. Just the town and the hills in background. No Owen. No Dad.

She could hear two distinct voices in the kitchen down the hall. Karla Parker, and Jack Parker.

Her smile widened. Her heart beat faster.

She heard her mother say something, and then heard her father laugh.

Tears welled up in her eyes at the sound of her father's laughter.

Get out there and see him! Tell him not to go to work, dork! she thought frantically. *This is why you risked your life! Go! Go! Go!*

She got to her feet and found that she was shaking. It was a mix of excitement and a high state of nerves, as though she'd drank three cups of coffee with two heaping spoons of hot chocolate mix in each one – a sugar high and caffeine rush.

She opened her bedroom door and now she could hear her parents even clearer. Molly walked down the very short hallway, feeling like her heart was going to explode.

"Good morning, Molly!" her mother said as soon as she caught sight of her daughter. Karla was standing by the kitchen counter with a spatula in her hand. She was making pancakes. Molly had been so preoccupied with waking up a year *before* she'd gone to sleep that she hadn't even registered the smell of cooking pancakes!

Her father was sitting at the table with his back to her. He turned to look at her as she came in, a mug of hot coffee in his hand. Jack's smile was sleepy and just as wonderful as she remembered it.

"Did you sleep well?" he asked, looking at her with a touch of concern.

"You have no idea," Molly replied shakily. A tear slid down her cheek. She walked up beside her father and threw her arms around him, almost knocking the mug out of his hand.

"Whoa, Molly!" Jack said, setting the mug down carefully. He hugged her back, a bit awkwardly as he was sitting and she was bending over a little. "What happened?"

Molly didn't even try to restrain herself. Tears fell as she began to relate her tale in a rapid string of words.

"I was visited by Father Time and the Creator a year from now. They said because I believed that things could change I could save you from the car accident that killed you!" She paused to breathe in deeply for a second before continuing. "I met Rheene and Gossamer and we were looking for Mother Nature because Neuos captured her and were holding her prisoner under the Tower of Raflure. We didn't know that at the time, but with Owen and Lorania and Mesna, who's a Giant, we made our way through the city (the Neuos had killed everyone there) and found Mother Nature and I gave her a new crystal sphere, and then the Creator brought the dead dragons back to life. And Father Time and Death said you were dead but not anymore, or something, and I could set the timeline right, and it's like I'm the only one who will know about it in this World. So," she breathed in again quickly, "you can't go to work today because that drunk driver will kill you! See? You gotta stay home and then everything will be alright!"

Jack Parker's face was blank for a moment. Then, a curious smile appeared on his lips as he looked into Molly's grey eyes. He lowered his eyes and saw the gold chain dangling from her neck – and then the golden pocket watch.

"Is that my pocket watch?" he asked in a strange voice. Molly could detect a little bit of fear in his words.

With tears in her eyes, a lump in her throat, and relief in her heart, she simply shook her head violently instead of trying to say anything.

Jack gave Karla a questioning glance. She quickly went into their bedroom and came out a few seconds later holding Jack's pocket watch in her hands. "Here's yours," she said, handing it to her husband.

Molly stood up, holding her pocket watch next to her father's.

Jack reached out to take ahold of Molly's pocket watch and turned it around so he could see the back of it.

"It's got your initials," her father said, his voice now touched with a bit of awe and sounding rather pleased. "M. M. P. See?"

Molly nodded. Her initials had not been there the entire time she'd journeyed with the watch. "I don't get it," Molly said. Then it hit her. "I guess that's because I'm a Dream Walker now! I think I can explain."

Jack Parker smiled warmly at his daughter and gave her arm a tender squeeze. "You don't have to explain it to *me*," he said, giving Molly a huge, exaggerated wink. "How do you think I got *my* pocket watch?"

And then…

…The Ghosts of Littletown continues in THE SEVEN…where the secret of the pocket watches is revealed, Brian Carter joins in the adventure, we discover who is responsible for unleashing the Neuos, and the Dream Walkers join forces to stop an invasion and fulfill an ancient prophecy.

CPSIA information can be obtained
at www.ICGtesting.com
Printed in the USA
LVHW031247220119
604790LV00002B/194/P